DON'T DRINK THE WATER

AN E. J. PUGH MYSTERY

SUSAN ROGERS COOPER

G.K. Hall & Co.   •   Chivers Press
Waterville, Maine USA   Bath, England

This Large Print edition is published by G.K. Hall & Co., USA
and by Chivers Press, England.

Published in 2001 in the U.S. by arrangement with
Avon Books, an imprint of HarperCollins Publishers, Inc.

Published in 2001 in the U.K. by arrangement with the author.

U.S. Softcover 0-7838-9521-6 (Paperback Series Edition)
U.K. Hardcover 0-7540-4631-1 (Chivers Large Print)
U.K. Softcover 0-7540-4632-X (Camden Large Print)

The text of this Large Print edition is unabridged.
Other aspects of the book may vary from the original edition.

Set in 16 pt. Plantin by Minnie B. Raven.

Printed in the United States on permanent paper.

British Library Cataloguing-in-Publication Data available

Library of Congress Cataloging-in-Publication Data

Cooper, Susan Rogers.
    Don't drink the water : an E.J. Pugh mystery /
Susan Rogers Cooper.
        p. cm.
    ISBN 0-7838-9521-6 (lg. print : sc : alk. paper)
    1. Pugh, E. J. (Fictitious character) — Fiction.   2. Saint John
(Antigua and Barbuda) — Fiction.   3. Women novelists —
Fiction.   4. Sisters — Fiction.   5. Large type books.   I. Title.
PS3553.O6235 D66 2001
813´.54—dc21   2001024814

DON'T DRINK
THE
WATER

To the Rogers clan:
Sissy, Greg, Karli, Dan,
and the Vins (Evin and Kevin)
and in loving memory of
Frank Rogers,
who took us all to paradise

ACKNOWLEDGMENTS

I would like first and foremost to thank my family, to whom this book is dedicated, for our incredible adventure on St. John, in the U.S. Virgin Islands. It's a shame E.J. and her family couldn't have as much fun as we did.

I'd like to thank the employees of the St. John Information Center in Cruz Bay, St. John, and the National Park Service, which oversees Virgin Islands National Park. I would also like to thank fellow writer Nancy Bell for her help with this manuscript, my research assistant Evin Cooper, Angel Powell for her contribution, and my husband Don Cooper (they also serve who only stand and wait). And, as always, a special thanks to my agent, Vicky Bijur, and my editor, Jennifer Sawyer Fisher.

ONE

"You've got the sunscreen?" I asked my husband.

"No, you have it."

"I gave it to you," I told him, gritting my teeth in my patience and understanding.

"You don't love us anymore, do you?" Bessie asked from her perch on the king-sized bed.

Willis and I looked at her. Bessie is very good at manipulating — as are most children — and we've been instructed to meet these attempts head-on.

"Yes, we love you," I said. "But that doesn't mean we can't take a vacation without you."

The look on her face was skeptical.

"We'll only be gone a little while," Willis said, which would have earned him a frown from Anne, our family therapist.

"You'll be with your grandmother and your brother and sister and all the dogs and cats and you'll have a wonderful time. And we have the right to go on a vacation. We're grown-ups," I said.

She scurried off the bed and headed for the

door. "Well, I hope you have a wonderful time. And don't worry about us." She sighed. "We'll be just fine."

She left, and Willis and I looked at each other. "We can't go," I said.

"Yes we can," he said.

"If we go we're terrible parents."

"If we don't go, we'll end up killing one of them. Then what kind of parents will we be?"

The thought of a long-term jail sentence was almost as appealing as the upcoming vacation. They both had their pros and cons. Excuse the pun.

The vacation had been my mother's idea — concocted a couple of months before at Christmas. My mother is the proud parent of four daughters who rarely speak to each other and have very little in common. Therefore she thought it would be a marvelous idea for the four of us and our spouses to spend "quality" time together somewhere where none of us could run away.

Preferably an island.

My brother-in-law Arlan — the Toad, as Willis and I not so affectionately call him — came up with St. John in the U.S. Virgin Islands. This he told my mother, who told me, and each of the other sisters in turn.

Although Willis and I have been able to plead poverty in the past when any kind of family adventure had come up, I'd made the unfortunate mistake of telling my mother about our

8

daughter Bessie's birth grandmother's legacy to us of $85,000. Most of it was gone now, but there was enough left for this little jaunt.

Why a family of redheaded women would want to spend any time on a tropical island is beyond me, but that's Arlan for you. Full of big ideas that never make a lot of sense.

But somehow my mother had cajoled us all into it, and now here Willis and I were, packing and deserting our three children.

"There it is," Willis said, pointing triumphantly at the SPF 50 sunscreen in my carry-on bag.

"I should have bought more than one tube," I said.

"Do you think it's possible that they might actually *sell* sunscreen on an island?" Willis tries for sarcasm, but I find him generally lacking in tone and quality.

"Maybe we can run by the drugstore on our way out of town," I suggested.

Willis looked at his watch. "It is now 9:03 a.m. Your parents expect us in Houston for lunch at twelve noon sharp. If we don't get out of this house in twelve minutes, we will be totally off schedule. I don't see any way we can make an unscheduled stop at the drugstore."

Don't ever marry an engineer — unless you are attracted to anal retentive behavior.

"I can't leave the house in twelve minutes," I said.

"E.J., you will," my husband declared.

9

"I don't have the cats' stuff together —"

"Graham's doing that."

"Oh, like he'll do it right! And I forgot to stop the paper —"

"I called them yesterday."

"The mail —"

"Will be picked up by Luna next door. You told me that yourself."

"Yeah, but what if she forgets?"

Willis threw a pair of underpants at me. "Pack this and shut up."

I sighed. I packed.

Somewhere along the way my mother picked up her own unique parenting skills. One of these was to endow each of her four daughters as special in some way. Elizabeth, the oldest, was the talented one. Nadine, the next, was the kind and nurturing one, Cheryl was the pretty one, and I was the smart one. All this did, of course, was tell us what we were not. Liz, Nadine, and I weren't pretty; Cheryl was stupid, unkind, and talentless.

The truly unfortunate part of this was Mother had a point — although this is arguably a chicken versus egg situation. Liz is now the director of a small theater company in Houston, while Nadine is a registered nurse who has worked in OB/GYN at Houston's Ben Taub Hospital for fourteen years, and Cheryl, like it or not, *is* pretty. Very pretty. And Liz, Nadine, and I have hated her for as long as she or we have been around. Okay, I made straight "A"s in high school and carried a 3.9 GPA throughout college. But again, that could have been environmental.

Liz and Nadine are two years apart and became friends early in life. Cheryl is four years younger than Nadine and I'm a year younger than Cheryl. It was mother's plan that Cheryl and I, like Liz and Nadine before us, be close friends as well as loving sisters.

Mother is the queen of organization and accessorizing. Not only does she have shoes and purses for every outfit, but when I was younger and she smoked, she had a cigarette case and lighter case to match every change of clothes.

Mother planned on two children. When Nadine was three and a half years old, Mother had an accident. I have no idea how this happened — no one does, but we suspect alcohol was involved — but Cheryl showed up. Being a regular subscriber to *Psychology Today*, Mother knew all about the trials and tribulations of middle children; therefore, she vowed to have an even number of children. Basically, if Cheryl hadn't been an accident, I never would have been conceived. In a way, I guess I actually owe Cheryl my life; I doubt if I've ever said thank you.

From the beginning Cheryl and I were barely sisters. Being only a year apart in age, we generally went to the same schools. Cheryl went off to high school while I was still in the eighth grade. The next year, when I got to high school, I found out my reputation preceded me — at least the part about the nonexistent herpes and the sixth toe.

Cheryl and I never ran with the same crowd, never went anywhere together, and shared a room only because we had to. Her side was filled with jars and lotions and pictures of supermodels, as bespoke her position as "the pretty one," while my side held only books and one poster of Einstein. My way of keeping up the "smart one" image.

We loathed each other.

By the time we were teenagers, Nadine and Liz were out of the house, so it was just the two of us, still crammed together in the same room because Mother thought it would generate a fondness for each other. As was often the case, Mother was wrong.

The highlight of my high-school life was when Cheryl got pregnant her senior year. The boy who knocked her up, Jason Johnson, captain of the football team, tried denying the baby was his, but when pressured by his parents and mine, 'fessed up. The two teenagers were led by their parents to the courthouse, where they were quietly married then went their separate ways.

I, of course, told anyone at school who would listen. I haven't got an exactly forgiving nature and the herpes thing still stung.

My nephew, William Jason Johnson, was born three weeks after Cheryl's graduation from high school. The father was not in attendance and, to my knowledge, has not seen Billy to this day.

Two husbands and three miscarriages later, Cheryl brought home Arlan Hawker, a long-haul trucker fifteen years her senior. While Cheryl was pregnant with their first daughter, Arlan ruptured several discs in his back while on the job. With the help of workman's compensation, rehabilitation, and a large loan from my father, Arlan went to dental tech school, where he learned to make dentures, partials, and bridges.

That was ten years and two daughters ago. Now he owns three dental labs in Houston, has a stock portfolio that would turn me green with envy — if I were the type to covet others' acquisitions — and built my sister the house she was born to be mistress of.

The fact that Arlan is the king of the rednecks and looks remarkably like a toad has never deterred my sister, who obviously married him for the long-haul trucking income and has stayed to reap the benefits of a change in fortune.

If this in any way comes across as though I'm not terribly fond of my sister Cheryl, well, I guess you're getting the drift.

I don't like Cheryl.

In fact, I loathe Cheryl.

Cheryl has strawberry blond hair — the color of a blush wine and the texture of silk. Her totally unfreckled skin is so translucent you can see a faint, oh so faint, blue veining underneath.

Cheryl never needed orthodonture, contacts, freckle cream, or a facial dipilatory.

As the runt of the litter, Cheryl was a perfect five-eight with a Barbie doll figure that erupted at the age of fourteen and hasn't changed an iota since.

My freshman year in high school, I had to walk into school next to her. I was certainly a vision at five-eleven, one hundred and ten pounds of elbows and knees, kinky carrot-red hair, and freckles the size of small change all over my body. And while Cheryl has remained at her perfect size eight, I had two babies and blossomed to a size fourteen (that I'll admit to).

Yes, I'm bitter. And no, I don't like Cheryl.

And yes, this is all my mother's fault. In her attempt to be a state-of-the-art, cutting-edge parent, she succeeded in breeding the most dysfunctional set of sisters in the greater Houston area.

I can hear you now — but what is Cheryl really like? Have I tried to discover her inner beauty, the kind, funny, thoughtful woman lurking under all that drop-dead gorgeousness?

Sorry. Cheryl's not terribly bright, has no sense of humor that I've ever been able to dis-

14

cover, is a barely adequate parent, and only gives to charity if it means climbing a step up the social ladder.

On the plus side, Cheryl's a fine little shopper. Give my sister four hours and a gold card and she could redecorate the White House. But only if she were moving in, of course.

Then there were the other two — Liz and Nadine.

You'd think since Liz and I were the artistic ones — she the director of a small theater company in Houston and me the author of twenty-four category romance novels — that we'd have a common bond. Think again. As far as my sister is concerned, I'm a hack. And you'll notice every time I mention her theater company, I use the pejorative "small."

Nadine, the kind and nurturing one, the one who has worked with the indigent and homeless of Houston for fourteen years, who has delivered hundreds of babies and cared for women in God-awful situations, came out of the closet five years ago. She now refers to me as a "breeder," even though she herself has two sons from a marital "mistake" that only lasted twenty years. She makes condescending, snide remarks in my presence about my lack of a "real job," small-town housewife status, and general "girliness," the last word in the world I'd personally use to describe myself. For four of the five years since coming out she's lived with a woman named Lorrette, whom I prefer almost any day to my own sister.

My mother is very proud of all her girls and tells us this continually, though not to our individual faces. Once a week on the phone she will extol the virtues of my three sisters to me, and I'm sure that the three of them, living near her in Houston, hear much more of my meager accomplishments than they'd like.

This is something that is not going to resolve itself. Ever. And spending a week stuck in each other's company was not going to help matters.

The problem was no one had the heart to explain this to Mother.

Therefore, we were all on our way to paradise for eight days of sunburn and snipes.

We loaded the minivan with kids, suitcases, cats, dog, and bottled water (we were driving less than a hundred miles to Houston, yet Willis, who was never actually in the Boy Scouts, has a "be prepared" fetish nonetheless), and drove from our house in Black Cat Ridge, a huge subdivision that is almost a town unto itself, south across the Colorado River into Codderville, the old town that had been sitting beside the Colorado long before the developers of Black Cat Ridge were a gleam in their great-granddaddies' eyes. Willis's mother, Vera, still lived in the same house where Willis grew up, and we were taking our children there for the eight days we planned on basking in dysfunc-

16

tion on the isle of St. John.

Willis had allowed ten minutes to unload the kids, dog, cats, and supplies before we had to hit the road to Houston. The goodbyes alone took me twenty-five minutes.

Willis was not amused.

"You'll call if anything comes up?" I asked Vera as we stood on the porch of her house, heading toward the van.

"Of course!" she said. "Now don't you worry! Everything's gonna be just fine."

Bessie took that moment to wrap her arms around my leg with a strength most ten-year-olds don't possess.

"Honey, let go," I said.

"No!" she shouted. "Don't go!"

Megan, never one to be outdone by her sister, ran up and grabbed my other leg. "Take us with you!" she begged.

Willis sighed and headed back up the stairs to the porch, attempting to dislodge his daughters' fingers from my legs.

"Girls, come on!" I said. "You're both going to have a great time with Grandma! You know that! Right, Grandma?" I pleaded, staring at Vera.

Vera sighed. "Well, you know, I never did go off and leave my children to anybody else's care, but those were different times —"

"Mother!" Willis chided. "Take the girls! Graham, get out here and help!"

Graham, thirteen, bored with the antics of

17

his sisters, and trying to start a rumor that he was an orphan, came to the front door. He casually leaned a shoulder against the door jamb, studying his sisters as they clung to my legs.

"That's a good look for you, Mom," he said, stuffing a Twinkie in his mouth.

"Share those with your sisters," I suggested.

"But Mom," he said, not moving from his perch, "you don't like it when we eat junk food." He grinned.

"Do you have any idea how grounded you are going to be —" Willis started.

Graham sighed and heaved himself away from the door jamb, breaking the second Twinkie in two. "Food, girls," he said, "come and get it."

Megan, who hadn't really been into the whole scene heart and soul, let go of my leg and headed for the Twinkie. Bessie, the drama queen, wasn't about to give up.

"Mama, I don't want to stay here! She's mean to me!"

"Who's mean to you?" I asked.

"Grandma!" she wailed.

Vera rolled her eyes. "Girl, you're telling lies again! I've never been mean to you in your whole life!" Vera said, hands on hips, finally ready to help — if only to clear her own good name.

"You make me wash dishes!" Bessie wailed, tears streaming down her face.

"Yeah, and for this I'm gonna make you dry 'em, too!" Vera said, prying Bessie's hands off my leg. "Say goodbye and let's go to Baskin Robbins."

The little hands loosened, Bessie sniffed, looked from me to her grandmother, glanced at her father, then headed in the house. "Bye!" she called over her shoulder.

Bribery is probably not the best solution, but sometimes you use what works.

We finally got in the van heading east, with Willis fuming and glancing at his watch every minute and a half, and me sniffling.

"Are you coming down with a cold?" he said, his voice dripping with a lack of compassion.

"I'm fine," I said, staring out the window at the Texas countryside rolling by.

"You've been away from the kids before, for God's sake," my husband said.

"I'm fine," I repeated.

Willis sighed.

I sighed.

He turned up the radio.

Our plane didn't leave Houston until 6:05 the next morning. Yes, a God-awful time for a plane, I'll agree. That's why we were getting to Houston today, so we could spend the night with my folks and leave early for the airport.

My parents live in West University Place, a small town actually within the central part of Houston. There are two such abnormalities in Houston — West University Place and Bellaire, both of which are terribly expensive and both of which are smack dab in the center of the city.

My mother's house, like my mother, is well organized and tastefully accessorized. It's a two-story New England salt box, with four rooms down and four rooms up, and an ivy-covered backyard. I try not to think about how much the house is worth in this day and age, especially when my mother pisses me off — which is just about any time I talk to her for more than three minutes at a stretch.

We got out of the car, taking small overnight bags with us, and were greeted at the door by Mother.

She kissed Willis, then me. "Oh, I wish you brought the children! We could take care of them as well as Vera, you know!" she said, ushering us into the living room.

"They have to go to school, Mother," I said, which she ignored.

My father was sitting in his recliner in front of the TV, his attention riveted by a basketball game. "The Rockets and Knicks," my father said to Willis as we walked in. "We're up three points. Second half."

Willis shook my father's hand and sat down on the couch. I kissed him on the cheek. "Hi, Daddy," I said.

"Hey little girl," he said, then added "move" as I walked in front of the TV.

I followed Mother into the kitchen. "I thought we were going out for lunch," I said, spying the kitchen table set and loaded with food.

"Well, I didn't count on the basketball game," Mother said and sighed. She shook her head. "It used to be just baseball and football. Now he's added basketball and hockey, and my God, Eloise, last week I saw him watching beach volleyball!"

I grinned. "Was it girls' volleyball?" I asked.

My mother rolled her eyes at me. "The way you talk!" she said, then handed me a bowl of potato salad to set on the table.

"I guess we'll need to set them up some TV trays in the living room," Mother said.

"I think they can handle that," I said, setting the dinnerware and napkins out in a buffet style.

Mother shook her head. "I swear you don't do anything for your husband, do you, Eloise? The way you keep a man, dear, is you wait on them every once in a while! Keeps 'em on their toes."

My given name is Eloise Janine, a name Willis refused to call me from almost the moment we met. I had no problem with that since I'd always hated my name anyway. Willis dubbed me E.J., and everyone in my life, with the exception of my parents and sisters, called me that.

I tried to ignore my mother, something I've been attempting without much success for close to — but not quite — forty years.

"I swear, your father wouldn't know what to do without me," Mother said. "I saw him looking at the washing machine one day, trying to figure it out, and I swear I was afraid he was fixing to leave me!" She laughed at her little joke.

"Go set up those TV trays, would you, dear?" Mother said, conveniently ignoring my earlier comment.

I went into the living room. "Mother said set up some TV trays if you want lunch," I said.

My father raised an eyebrow and grinned at me. "Somehow I doubt those were her exact words," he said. With his eyes still on the TV, he said to Willis, "Son, set those trays up for me, wouldja?"

Willis stuck his tongue out at me; I returned the face and went back into the kitchen.

The rest of the day went on unrelentingly in that manner. We all sat in the living room watching TV. After the game, my father showed off his new satellite dish by jumping through the hundreds of channels until he came to the Game Show Network. "Wait'll you see this," he said to Willis. "They got reruns of 'Match Game.'"

Sure enough, they did.

Mother sat in her chair knitting, Daddy slapped his knee at Gene Rayburn's thirty-year-old wit, and Willis and I kicked each other like teenagers waiting for Mom and Dad to go to bed so we could neck.

We went out to dinner at five o'clock. I was still full from lunch, but that didn't seem to be the point.

"We always eat early," Mother said. "It's better for your father's digestion. Besides, if you wait any later, the lines are terrible! I, for one, do not intend to stand in line for my supper!"

We went to a diner that had a senior citizen Saturday night special (hamburger pattie/ chicken breast, mashed potatoes/macaroni and cheese, salad/soup, a dinner roll, iced tea/coffee, and cherry/apple pie for dessert) for $5.95 plus tax and tip. Willis and I opted for hamburgers and we were home and in bed by eight o'clock. Talk about your uptown Saturday night.

The next morning, although we arose at four-thirty, Mother had beaten us to it. She was in the kitchen frying bacon when we came down. Daddy was at the table reading the paper. "You see what that Democratic government you put in office is up to now, Willis?" he said, pointing at the front page. "Now when Nixon was in office —"

"Daddy!" I interrupted.

Willis kissed my mother on the cheek. "We don't have time for breakfast, Louise. Gotta hit the road."

"For God's sake, Willis, it's not even five o'clock!" I protested.

"Yeah, and the plane leaves at 6:05! We need to be there at least an hour ahead of time," he said.

"Now when Nixon was in office, we could get to a plane with a minute to spare —"

"Daddy!" I interrupted.

We grabbed our bags and headed for the minivan, Mother and Daddy walking with us, while Daddy explained the problems with the present administration.

"It's you Democrats, Willis. You're lazy!"

Willis grimaced. He was usually up to these political debates with my father, but the clock was ticking and Willis has little humor when it comes to being late.

"And you Republicans are money-grubbers," I said, trying to keep the Pugh hand in since Willis seemed to be refusing to play.

"Nothing wrong with some fiscal responsibility, little girl," Daddy said. "You Democrats might try it sometime."

I kissed my father on the cheek. "You're old and conservative, Daddy. That's your problem," I said, sliding into the passenger side of the car.

"Old? Who you calling old?" Daddy started, but Willis turned the car on, grinding the gears.

"We've got to go, Henry," he said, backing out.

"You two be careful and have a wonderful time! And be nice to your sisters, Eloise, do you hear me?" Mother yelled, almost running to keep up with the car as Willis backed out of the driveway.

"Goodbye!" Willis yelled, as he rolled up the window and flew down the quiet street where I grew up.

"You are so rude!" I said.

"Don't start!" he said. "Do you realize how late we're going to be?"

I ignored him and looked out the window at the darkness. He was really getting on my last nerve.

We pulled into the long-term parking lot on the road to Houston Intercontinental Airport at 5:25 a.m. Our plane was to leave at 6:05 a.m. Willis was in a total panic. The sky was still dark, the only light coming from the streetlights and a shuttle coming straight at us.

Willis jumped out of the minivan and screamed at me, "Grab that shuttle!"

I rolled my eyes and wiggled my fingers at the shuttle driver who was pulling up to our spot without any help from me.

"Grab some bags, for God's sake!" Willis said.

I put my hands on my hips and stared at him. "If you don't calm down, I'm not going!"

"Face it, you don't want to go anyway and you'll use any excuse not to! Now grab a damned bag!"

I got two rolling suitcases and it took every fiber of control I had left not to hit my husband in the head with one. He piled the luggage onto the shuttle, muttering under his breath the whole time. The shuttle driver wore a tolerant semismile.

Everyone else on the shuttle seemed either bored (the business people) or excited — other vacationers like ourselves. We were the exception. All decked out in vacation wear, both scowling for all we were worth. I couldn't help thinking this didn't bode well for the next eight days.

We got to our gate with twenty minutes to spare. This did not please Willis, which he explained at some length to my brother-in-law Larry, Liz's husband, the minute we spotted them sitting there waiting for us.

I hugged Liz and Larry, spotted Nadine and her partner Lorrette sitting a couple of chairs down, and hugged them too. We do this. No one knows why, but it's one of those things Mother always insisted on. It made us *look* like we really cared.

Liz is taller than me at six foot one, and has weighed 135 pounds since puberty. She's stoop-shouldered, wears glasses, has hair the color of an old, beat-up penny, and is the mother of two daughters, both of whom have made her a grandmother. Her husband Larry is a dentist. He's the same height as Liz and has graying blond hair and a quick smile. The smile never seems to mean anything, and it comes out at the strangest times, but it is still a nice smile.

My sister Nadine, although taller than Cheryl, is still another short one. She's five foot nine and weighs — well, she's not telling. If faced with the jaws of hell for the knowledge, she'd go willingly and keep her secret. Let's just

26

say Nadine makes me look and feel thin. Not an easy task to accomplish. The two of us share the same color of carrot-red hair, and, if possible, she has more and larger freckles than I do. Even that has not managed to bond us as sisters.

Her partner Lorrette is shorter, a little thinner, has frosted hair cut short, and isn't sure after four years with my sister whether she likes any of us or not. I don't really blame her. I'm not sure if I like her either — and I know I don't like the rest of them.

Nadine said, "Can you believe this? Eight days on an island with Arlan Hawker? I'd rather Larry gave me a root canal with no anesthetic."

Larry flashed his sister-in-law a quick, meaningless smile while still listening to Willis's tirade.

"Did you bring sunscreen?" I asked her.

"Are you kidding? Twelve tubes of SPF 35. Cost almost as much as the damned plane ticket!"

"Wow, twelve?" I said, shooting my husband a withering glance. And he begrudged me buying one extra little tube!

Lorrette, who was olive-complected, smirked. "I'm thinking of getting a tan," she said.

Nadine and I had a rare instance of bonding as we glared at her partner.

"What is Willis going on about?" my other sister Liz asked me.

I shrugged. "We weren't three hours early for

the plane," I explained.

Liz rolled her eyes. "Yeah, well, we've been here since four o'clock this morning. Larry likes to have plenty of time to sit in airports. I guess he just doesn't get enough of plastic chairs at his dental office."

"Now does everybody realize that since Cheryl and Arlan are getting to the house before us, they're gonna get the best room?" Nadine demanded, hands on ample hips.

"Of course they are," Liz said, rolling her eyes some more. "Why do you think Arlan took this whole thing over? If he's in charge, he and Cheryl get all the goodies!"

"How many bedrooms does this house have?" I asked, beginning to worry about having to sleep in a hammock on the deck.

"Oh, there are four bedrooms," Nadine said, "but that's not the point!"

"No, the point is," Lorrette jumped in, "that only one of them is a master suite and you *know* who's going to get that!"

She and Nadine shared a disgusted look.

"Well, hell, as long as we get a king-sized bed," Liz said, "I don't really care."

"Yeah, well I'll bet the only king-sized bed's in the master suite!" Lorrette said.

Liz rolled her eyes and breathed in my ear, "It's going to be a *lovely* week!"

I figured we were off to a fine start. Things could only go downhill from here.

TWO

St. John in the U.S. Virgin Islands is one of those places that you basically "can't get to from here." Here being anywhere, actually. Except maybe one of the other islands.

We flew from Houston to Miami, sat for two hours in the airport, got on a plane for St. Croix, got off that plane, and three hours later got on another plane — this one a propeller job with enough seats for us and a few more stragglers — to St. Thomas. It was the middle of the night and we still weren't in St. John. We took a taxi from the airport to Charlotte Amalie, a very dark town (it was almost ten o'clock and there weren't a lot of lights), where we caught the last ferry going to St. John.

"Couldn't Arlan find a place more isolated?" Nadine said, using her own brand of sarcasm. I silently declared myself still queen of that particular form of wit.

This is when I discovered my previously unknown phobia of boats. We gave all our luggage over to a man we hoped had something to do with the ferry — the island patois he spoke was so thick that I, personally, had no idea what he was actually saying — and climbed aboard, all going to the open-air top deck for a better view of the black expanse of sea and sky.

Everything was fine until we got about a quarter mile out and the swells started. The boat rocked from one side to another. This is fine when you're in a small sailboat or motor-boat, close to the water, riding with the waves. Not so in a top-heavy ferry. People were sliding on the benches, laughing as they were unable to hold on, rolling from one side of the large top deck to the other.

I was not laughing. I was terribly close to peeing in my pants. I grabbed hold of Willis and shouted in his ear, above the noise of the ferry boat engine, "We're all going to die!"

He patted my hand. "With any luck," he said, and gave me a smile.

I decided he had a point, considering that the two-hour layover in Miami had been two hours of Lorrette bitching because she couldn't find anyplace to smoke, Larry coughing and sneezing from what he claimed were his "Miami allergies," and Willis still mad at me for "barely" making the plane in Houston. Hey, we *made* the plane, right?

Liz and Nadine, who had been great friends growing up, were barely speaking now since Nadine's leap from the closet. Working in the-ater as Liz did, I doubted she could have many problems with gay men and women and still be in the business. But this may have been something more personal. A sister thing. A "why didn't I know this from the day you were born?" kind of thing. Whatever it was, I thought a couple of years of therapy might help, but I doubted they cared enough to deal with it.

When I had my brainstorm and bought a deck of cards at the airport bookstore in hopes of whiling away the time, our plane was called.

Once in St. Croix, we walked around the open-air airport, seeing glimpses of the magnificent Caribbean but unable to reach it due to the high fences that separated the airport from the beaches.

It was early March, and back home it could have been very cold or a warm spring day, depending on the Texas weather's mood. In St. Croix it was hot. Beautiful, but hot.

We finally found an air-conditioned cafe inside the airport, bought Coronas all around, and played cards for two hours straight. Willis hates playing cards and bitched the entire time, Nadine tended to cheat, and Liz couldn't tell the difference between the "shovels" and "those clover-looking things."

Which eventually brought us back to the ferry. When it finally began to slow and I could see lights ahead, thoughts of living through the journey began to emerge. One of those thoughts was that I was only a short time away from a warm welcome from my sister Cheryl.

We were a mixed bag getting off the ferry. Spring-breaking college students in jeans and backpacks, globe-trotting seniors in Bermuda shorts, hats, and camera bags, and islanders coming back from what appeared to be a beauty contest on the bigger island. The winner, wearing a floor-length evening gown with a sash proclaiming her Island Queen, was in front of me with her entourage: five other teenaged girls, a couple of boys, and an older woman, all beaming at the crowd waiting on the dock, stomping and waving their hands and cheering their queen.

The six of us rescued our luggage and maneuvered around the islanders, heading for the end of the dock where cars, trucks, and buses waited.

Tagging along behind, I managed to roll one of my suitcases over the sandal-clad foot of a young black woman.

"Oh, I'm sorry," I said, trying to get my suitcase off her foot.

She ducked her head, a long, dark, corn-rowed weave covering her face, and quickly dodged me, not saying a word.

I hurried to catch up with my party, who were standing at the entrance to the dock, looking around.

There was no sign of Cheryl or Arlan.

"They're late!" Nadine declared to anyone listening.

"You're surprised?" Lorrette said, under her breath.

"Cheryl wouldn't be on time for her own funeral," Liz said.

I sat down on the larger piece of luggage, knowing we could be there for a while.

"What's the telephone number at the house?" Larry asked. He pointed to the left. "I see a payphone over there. I'll call. They might not know what time the last ferry gets in."

"They could have checked!" Nadine groused.

"I don't have the number," Liz said. She looked at me. "Do you have it?"

I shrugged. "I don't even know the address," I said.

"Well, this is ridiculous!" Nadine said. "Didn't she give anybody the number?"

No one admitted it.

"This is so like Cheryl!" Liz said. "To just leave us standing around here like idiots!"

Larry smiled. "Oh, honey," he said, "it's gonna be —"

"What do we do? Call the police?" Lorrette asked.

"If we don't even know the address —" Nadine said, throwing her hands up in the air.

It was past eleven o'clock at night and we had all been up since very early that morning, which is my subtle way of excusing our catty — okay, bitchy — behavior.

I saw Willis looking at his watch. "Let's give

them fifteen minutes, then we'll look for a hotel."

"Good God, Willis," Nadine said, rolling her eyes. "It's spring break! Where do you think we're going to find rooms for all of us!"

"Well, Nadine," Willis said, grinding his teeth, "we might have to double up, mightn't we?"

"Don't you take that tone with me, mister!" Nadine said, getting in Willis's face.

Larry smiled. "Hey, gang, there's a bar over there," he said pointing. "Anybody want a drink?"

Everybody turned and glared at Larry. His smile didn't waver.

A huge black Land Rover came to a screeching halt practically on Lorrette's toes, blocking the dock exit, and turned off its engine, right in front of a large NO PARKING sign. My brother-in-law Arlan Hawker got out of the Land Rover.

"Hey, guys!" he yelled, coming over and grabbing Liz and me together in a big bear hug. We both towered over him so that his nose was firmly on one of my breasts and his ear on one of Liz's.

Liz and I managed to extricate ourselves and he went for Nadine and Lorrette. Nadine, having known him longer, managed to sidestep the hug; Lorrette, however, got the full brunt of the Toad from Hell treatment. If she hadn't already been gay before that assault, she definitely would have been after.

Willis grabbed Arlan's arm, pulling him away from Lorrette and pumping his hand. "Hey, Arlan," he said, grinning like Larry, "good to see you."

Arlan returned the pumping action and slapped Willis on the shoulder. "Hey, man, good to see you, too! We were afraid you two weren't going to be able to make it! Glad you were able to find the money. But if you need a loan while we're here, you just holler, fella, you got me?"

Willis stiffened, the smile hardening on his face. "We'll be fine, Arlan, thank you."

"Where's Cheryl?" Liz asked.

"Back at the house fixing up a nice dinner for y'all," Arlan said, pumping Larry's hand. "Good to see you, boy."

"You too, Arlan," Larry said.

Liz and I exchanged a look. Nadine and Lorrette exchanged a look. No one needed to mention that our sister Cheryl couldn't heat up a microwave dinner with the instructions printed on the back of her eyelids, let alone "fix up a nice dinner" for eight.

"Whata y'all think of this?" Arlan said, pointing to the Land Rover. "All they got around here is them little bitty Suzuki SUV things. Had to have this baby brought over from another island. Had to pay an arm and leg, but you want the best, it's gonna cost ya, huh, Willis?"

Willis ignored him and started grabbing luggage. With all our stuff in the Land Rover, it was a tight squeeze getting seven people in, but we managed.

"Now this island's like in England. They drive on the wrong side of the road, but it's no big deal. Specially when you're driving something as big as this old thing," Arlan said, starting the engine, hitting the horn, and turning the big car in a tight fast circle.

We drove through the dark night, not seeing much of anything but a few lights and the narrowness of the roads. I began to understand the wisdom of those "little bitty Suzuki things." It didn't matter whether we were supposed to drive to the right or the left — Arlan did neither. He drove straight down the middle, hitting his horn and laughing whenever another car came by.

"Arlan!" Liz yelled from the front seat.

"Ah, don't worry, honey. I been here one whole day and these people are getting used to me. They know to get out of Arlan Hawker's way. I wasn't a long-haul trucker for twenty years for nothing!"

We went up twisting, night-dark roads, turning here and there, able to get an occasional glimpse of the dark Caribbean below us with the dots of light from boats anchored in the harbor.

After turning on two more roads, Arlan said, "Now, here's the fun part," as he took a sharp turn and the Land Rover careened straight down a narrow, cobblestone driveway. Arlan slammed on the brakes less than a foot from the side of a massive wall.

He turned off the engine and bailed from the car. "We're home, kiddies. Y'all unpack this thing then I'll park it. It's a bear to park, I'm telling ya."

A door opened and Cheryl stepped out onto the cobblestone surround. She was a vision with the light from the house shining behind her. I ignored her and headed to the back of the Land Rover for the luggage.

"Hey, y'all," she said, coming up to hug Willis and Larry first. Her voice was the only thing not natural about Cheryl's beauty. It was a low, husky, Kathleen Turner type of voice, and I knew just how studied it was. When she'd left home at the age of nineteen, leaving one-year-old Billy to the care of my parents, she left with a high-pitched, rather nasal east Texas drawl. When she returned two years later with Arlan Hawker, it was Kathleen Turner time.

But enough about my sister. Let me tell you about the house. The cobblestone surround led to a double front door that led, in turn, to a landing built of teak. Skylighted atriums filled with exotic flowers were on either side of the entry. The landing ended at a rail overlooking the massive living room on the floor below. The landing divided at that point — to the left the master suite that took the entire left side of the

upper story, and to the right two smaller bedrooms. Teak stairways led down from each side
to the floor below.

The Spanish-tiled living room had floor to
two-story-high windows looking out at the bay
beyond. It was furnished with thick oriental
rugs, suede couches and chairs, the largest-
screen TV I'd ever seen, and a CD unit that
could play one hundred CDs.

To the right, under the two bedrooms above,
was the kitchen/dining area, the kitchen complete with Sub-Zero refrigerator, a marble and
chrome stovetop, a wall of ovens, and enough
toys to keep a gourmand happy indefinitely.
The connecting dining area was furnished with
a large table, sofa, big-screen TV, and a wraparound bar extending from the stovetop that sat
eight easily. To the left of the living room was
the other master suite. This house came
equipped with two.

The house was designed as three octagon-
shaped areas — the living area, the master
suites area, and the kitchen/dining area. The
two-story-high living area rose to a teak-lined
peaked ceiling.

The deck could be reached from the downstairs master suite, the living room, or from two
places in the kitchen area. It covered the entire
width of the house and offered an incredible
view of the bay and the boats anchored there, a
rocky beach just beyond, lush tropical plants,
the colors and identities of which I couldn't

discern in the dark, and a double-decker swimming pool with a slide connecting the two levels. At least this is what Arlan told us. We'd have to wait for the light of day to see some of it for ourselves, but still, it was no wonder this house was costing us over $1,000 a day.

There was another couple sitting in the living room. Arlan introduced them as Marge and Bud George.

"Small world, huh?" Arlan said. "Come all the way out here and who's the first people we run into on the very first day? Texans! That's who!"

Bud laughed uproariously and held out his hand first to Willis then to Larry. "We're from Snyder, Texas. Way out west, you know it?" He pointed out toward the bay. "We're renting us a cabin cruiser, got it anchored out there in the bay."

These two were the ones who gave Texans a bad name. They definitely should have stayed home rather than wander the world perpetuating the Texas stereotype.

Bud was about five foot nine, stocky, and wore his beer gut like a badge of honor. He had on orange Bermuda shorts, white crew socks pulled up to mid-calf, black rubber sandals, a very expensive-looking but still ugly Hawaiian shirt, and a straw cowboy hat, the band of which was studded with trinkets from around the world. He wore a diamond pinky ring on his right hand, an emerald lodge ring on his left, and a gold nugget bracelet on the wrist not occupied by the gold and diamond Rolex.

I couldn't help but wonder how his wife Marge was able to fit all the makeup needed to create the face she presented to us on a boat. Her hot pink ruffled, off-the-shoulder blouse revealed entirely too much darkly tanned, leathery skin, and her obviously dyed blond hair needed conditioning in the worst way. Her white pants were so tight I worried about her ability to breathe, and they showed perfectly the outline of her bikini underwear. What jewelry was left in the shop after her husband got through she was wearing — diamonds on her ears, neck, wrists, fingers, ankles, and toes.

"Ol' Arlan and Cheryl been telling us all about y'all," Marge said, pumping the hands of the women in the group. "We're just so excited to meet all y'all, aren't we, Bud?"

"Boy howdy, yeah," Bud said, grinning. "Come to a place like this, best thing in the world is to find something from home. Specially around here, what with all the darkies."

Darkies? I asked myself. I didn't think I'd ever actually heard that word used in conversation, thank God.

The dinner that my sister Cheryl had been slaving over was take-out deli, but it did smell and look delicious. Arlan asked the Georges to join us.

"Wish we could, Arlan, I know Cheryl here's been slaving away in that galley in there," Bud said, laughing at his own wit, "but we got to meet some other friends in Cruz Bay for dinner tonight. Y'all gotta meet them! Norm and Ellen Bernstein? He's a Jew, but he seems real nice."

As we waved goodbye, Marge came up to me and took both my hands in hers. "Arlan tells me you write romances. I just love romances! That's all I ever read! We gotta talk! See if I read any of your books! I'm just so excited to meet a real, live arthur."

I tried not to meet Willis's eye, while at the same time I tried not to correct her English. It was difficult. "Sure," I said, wincing. "We can talk anytime."

"Why, you are just so gracious I can't believe my ears! Bud, did you hear that?" she said, turning to her husband. "I told you romance writers were the nicest people in the whole world!" She turned back to me. "I just knew y'all had to be! How can you write such beautiful stuff and be mean, huh? Answer me that!"

I smiled.

Arlan walked them out to the deck where the two headed for their dinghy tied up at the rock beach, while Willis punched me in the ribs. I stepped on his toe to shut him up.

" 'Fore we get down to the groceries," Arlan said, coming back in, "we gotta figure out the sleeping arrangements. Me and Cheryl took the upstairs master suite. Now there's another one downstairs, then there's a nice-sized room faces the water, but it shares a bath with a little bitty room faces the front of the house. Now the way I figure it, whoever takes the little room should pay less than the rest of us. What you say, Willis? Y'all want the little room?"

I could see Willis's chest puff up in readiness to a response. Luckily, Lorrette jumped in first. "We'll take it, if it means paying less. That okay, honey?" she asked Nadine.

Nadine shrugged. "Sure. This thing's costing too damned much as it is."

"That's fine," Willis said. "We'll take the room that shares a bath with y'all, if that's okay."

Liz grinned. "I guess that means we get the other master suite," she said as she pushed Larry up the stairs to get their luggage and bring it down, presumably before Willis changed his mind.

I went up with Willis to get our luggage. "Why couldn't we take the other master suite?" I whispered to him, my teeth clinched.

"I don't want to talk about it," Willis said, grabbing luggage and slamming it into our room.

I let out a whistle when I saw our room. It may not have been a master suite, but it was nothing to sneeze at. The room was octagan-shaped with windows on six of the eight sides of the room. I ran to one of the windows and opened it. The sound of the surf and sea filled the room. The smell of salt water and brine drifted up. The teak ceiling came to a point about a story and a half up. There was a queen-sized bed, two easy chairs, an air conditioner, and built-in dressers. The bath we shared with Nadine and Lorrette had a sunken tub and an outdoor shower. I was thinking seriously of never going home again.

I woke up the next morning at sunrise. Willis was sleeping soundly beside me. A warm breeze was blowing in through the open window and I could hear the far-off clang of metal against metal as the sailboats moored in the bay rocked on the water.

I got up quickly and went to the windows. Unbelievable. I snuck out through the bathroom to the outdoor shower, where there was a rock staircase leading down to the lower level of the deck and pool area. Beyond the pool was a waist-high rock planter stuffed with tropical plants and flowers. In front of me was the bay, the water as blue and clear as Mel Gibson's eyes. Dozens of boats rocked in the gentle swells of the bay, everything from a very modern, sleek sailboat with a conical-shaped metal mast to an old and slightly disreputable-looking schooner, painted in peeling shades of red and yellow.

Straight across the water the land rose steeply with houses painted brightly in blues and pinks and whites, holding on miraculously to the side of the hill, half hidden by thick, green vegetation. The land jutted out into the water at the head of the bay, and from there I could see nothing but the Caribbean, shining blue and mauve and gray in the rising light.

As the sun rose, the colors of the bougain-villea and hibiscus came to life: flaming hot pinks, deep crimsons, and blazing whites. As the house behind me slept, so did most of the boats in the bay. On one a man was busy with his morning chores, whistling an off-key tune. Although he was a good ways from me, the water carried the song to me — "Yesterday," by the Beatles. I smiled.

A woman walked along the rock-strewn beach in front of our house. She was dark-skinned, with long, multi-braided hair flowing behind her, a white, gauzy dress whipping in the wind. She looked like she should be in a douche commercial.

As she neared, she spotted me. I waved, but she scurried on, making me wonder if the beach was private and belonged only to this house. Maybe she'd been afraid I was going to give her trouble for walking on my beach. I grinned. My beach. Not bad.

I was in paradise and no amount of sibling bickering was going to ruin it for me. The night before had been about what I'd expected. For the first twenty minutes or so, everyone acted like we were having a grand old time, pleased to be in each other's company. After that, the first bickering started.

Cheryl made a snide remark about Lorrette — a person to whom she has never spoken directly. Nadine defended her partner. Liz stepped in to defuse the situation and ended up getting the brunt of it from both Cheryl and Nadine.

Arlan made four — count 'em four — nasty comments about Willis's income. Lorrette refused to eat the dinner Cheryl had "prepared."

Through it all Larry smiled and I found a bottle of island rum very much to my liking.

But in the light of day, the beautiful light of day falling on this island paradise, there was no way I was going to let my sisters get to me. I took off my pajamas and slid into the lower level of the pool. I hadn't been skinny-dipping since the early seventies, and as the water and early morning sun touched those parts of my body most often reserved for my private bed and bath, I remembered why I liked it so much. I was invisible from the bay and the beach, both at much lower levels than the deck and pool area, and it was still very early. I knew no one in the house would catch me, so I lay on my back, feeling the early morning sun on my face and breasts, closed my eyes and floated.

And didn't feel the least bit guilty about anything — not even having abandoned my children.

Water splashed me in the face and I rolled over quickly, immersing myself in the water of the pool. Coming up for air, covering myself as best I could with one arm over my breasts and the other for my privates, I peeked to see who was there.

No one. I sank low in the water, only my nose and eyes in the air. Someone had been there. There was no way I got splashed by nothing. Then I felt it. A pinch on my butt. I whirled around, only to see Willis come up out of the water, laughing.

"Got ya," he said.

"Shhh," I whispered, putting my arms around his neck. "Don't wake up anybody else."

He was as naked as I was; it was then that I noticed the heap of his pajama bottoms next to mine on the edge of the pool.

"You're naked," I whispered in his ear.

"So are you," he said.

Then we stopped talking for a while.

We got out of the pool and to our room only moments before the rest of the house began to rise. We took a shower in the outdoor facility, giggling over our naughtiness.

"Is this place beautiful or what?" I said.

"It's great," he agreed.

"You think you can ignore Arlan long enough to enjoy yourself?" I asked.

He scrubbed my back. "Naw. I'm just going to kill him," he said.

"Okay," I said, leaning into his hands. "Sounds fine to me."

"Cheryl should enjoy the insurance," he said.

"Um," I said.

When we got downstairs, Nadine was busily breaking eggs into a bowl while Liz fried bacon. I grabbed a loaf of bread and headed for the toaster.

Larry and Arlan were outside on the deck, Arlan pointing out things of interest in the bay, and Lorrette sat at the table drinking coffee and reading a brochure on the island.

"Did you know that they didn't allow cars on St. John until the early fifties? Oh, here's something interesting," she said. "Slaves were brought here for the sugar plantations and rum mills, right? Well, in 1733, they revolted and held the island for six months!" She read some more. "This was in Coral Bay. We should go there."

Cheryl was nowhere to be seen, which was quite all right with me.

Willis grabbed a cup of coffee and joined Lorrette at the table.

"And the national park," Lorrette read, "which takes up about three-quarters of the island, was formed with the help of one of the Rockefellers. Lawrence."

When breakfast was ready, we called the guys in and Liz asked Arlan where Cheryl was.

"Getting some extra beauty sleep," he said, and chuckled. "Not that she needs any, huh, gals?"

We ignored him and ate, talking about what we planned to do with the day.

"Y'all bring your snorkeling equipment?"

Arlan asked. "Reason I'm asking, 'cause if you didn't, there's a shop on the way into Cruz Bay rents all that stuff. And there's another place does scuba if you're into that."

"Snorkeling sounds good," I said.

"We can go out here," Arlan said, pointing to our rocky beach, "or drive to one of the better beaches. According to the brochures, they got some kick-ass beaches around here. You girls bring your sunscreen?"

"They got some really nice hiking trails," Lorrette said, holding up her brochure. "And there are a couple with sugar mill ruins on them. That should be interesting."

"What about shopping?" Liz asked.

Arlan guffawed. "Now ain't that just like a woman? Come to an island paradise and wants to go shopping!"

Liz sent her brother-in-law a withering look.

Larry smiled. "We have to buy the grandkids some things or we won't be allowed home, huh, honey?"

"Whatever," Liz said, studying the dregs of breakfast left on her plate.

"Well, there's all sorts of shops in Cruz Bay, and further up the island, there's Coral Bay, where the fort that Lorrette was talking about is. I hear they all got shops. Most of this island's a national park though. Serious shopping, you gotta go to St. Thomas," Arlan said.

"Well, I'm with Liz. We need to get the kids some things. And I love to check out little, eclectic shops," I said, trying to calm my sister down.

"Why don't we rent our own car," Willis suggested. "One of those Suzuki SUVs, so we can go somewhere else if we want?"

"Good idea," Liz said. "That way we won't be beholden to you, Arlan," she said, giving him a look that I'm sure has sent more than one would-be actor scurrying off to tech school.

Cheryl took that moment to make her appearance, and if there's one thing my sister Cheryl can do, it's make an appearance.

Her strawberry blond hair was piled in a very artistically haphazard fashion on the top of her head. She was wearing a dark green print bikini that no woman her age should have been able to pull off. Cheryl, of course, pulled it off. A matching green, fringed shawl was tied around her hips at an angle, exposing one long, gorgeous leg and just a little of the French cut bikini bottom. Her feet were clad in two-inch high sandals that appeared to only connect to her foot by one little strap around the big toe. Her makeup was so artfully done it appeared as if she weren't wearing any — and if she weren't, then I planned on killing myself later that day.

I heard masculine intakes of breath and decided not to look in case one of those had come from my husband.

"Morning all," Kathleen — I mean Cheryl — said as she rested one lovely hip on the stool next to Arlan's.

"Hey, babe," Arlan said, leaning forward to kiss her lightly on the cheek. "Looking good."

Cheryl smiled. "Beautiful day," she said.

"We were talking about where we wanted to go today," Nadine said, "and about maybe renting another car, or even two. That way we can all do whatever we want."

Cheryl pouted. "The whole idea of this trip was so that we could do things together," she said. "You know, a bonding experience."

Larry smiled, Willis cleared his throat, and Lorrette got up and walked out to the deck. Liz, Nadine, and I looked at each other, then anywhere else we could think of. I was very close to hysterical laughter.

I was nine years old, which would have made Cheryl ten, Nadine fourteen, and Liz sixteen. Our parents went to the neighbors' one evening and left Liz in charge of the rest of us. That was the evening she sat us down and explained French kissing.

"The boy sticks his tongue in your mouth," she said.

I thought I was going to gag. "Yuck!" I said. "Why?"

Liz shrugged. "They like it."

Cheryl was pensive. "They like it?" she asked.

Liz nodded. "They like it even better when you stick your tongue in their mouth."

"Double yuck!" I said.

"How do you do it?" Cheryl asked.

Liz demonstrated, using the space between her

thumb and forefinger as the boy's mouth.

"Gross!" I said. "And boys really like this?" I demanded, thinking of my friend Mike and knowing he wouldn't like it at all if I tried sticking my tongue in his mouth. And I knew he wouldn't want to stick his in mine!

"It's sorta like sex," Liz said.

Well, she had me there.

Nadine nodded. "That makes sense," she said.

Cheryl and I looked at each other and tried not to admit we had no idea what they were talking about.

Later that night in the bedroom we shared, Cheryl and I discussed the revelation we'd gotten earlier from Liz.

"I'm never gonna do that!" I declared.

"What?" Cheryl asked.

"Stick my tongue in some boy's mouth! Or let him stick his in mine! Yuck!"

"Well, Liz says that's what they want."

"So what?" I demanded.

Cheryl sat up in bed, her pretty face serious. "We're supposed to please them," she said. "I mean, a woman is supposed to please her husband, right? And we're gonna be women, right?"

I was confused. "Who says women are supposed to please their husbands?" I asked, thinking my daddy didn't look all that pleased most of the time.

"God," Cheryl said.

As far as I knew, the only thing God wanted from me was not to throw like a girl and to give a dime of my weekly dollar allowance to the collection plate at Sunday school.

I shook my head. "I don't think so," I said.

Cheryl was adamant. "That's what I heard at church," she said, "so it must be true. And I vow right now to stick my tongue in every boy's mouth I can until I find the right one!"

I would say that is probably exactly what my sister Cheryl did, my point being that as a group, we don't bond well.

THREE

"Well, 'fore we fight it out about cars and all, we got some house business to take care of," Arlan said. "The rental agent that showed me and Cheryl around when we first got here told us some things. For one, this island doesn't have a reservoir and water's sorta scarce. This house's got a cistern, right here in the living room," he said.

He walked over by the double doors leading out to the deck and, with Larry's help, pulled up a trap door. We all gathered around to look. Water gently lapped against the sides of the approximately five-foot by five-foot hole in the floor of the living room, about two feet down from the line I could see that it read "FULL."

"This thing holds rainwater, when there is some, and it gets filled up like once a week from a truck comes over from the big island," Arlan said. "So we gotta watch our water consumption." He put the lid back down. "Also, we're responsible for the garbage. There's a communal Dumpster down the road a ways where we need to take our garbage, probably like once a day. Also, they got a maid comes like only once a week, so we gotta clean up after ourselves. Now, Eloise, you should be used to that, but poor Cheryl here's gonna be really roughin' it!" he said, putting his arm around his wife and giving her a sloppy kiss. Cheryl smiled tolerantly. I didn't.

"Well, I guess that means we'll need to be careful about laundry and showers," Nadine said.

Willis grinned at me. "We can always rinse off in the pool."

"What *about* the pool water?" Lorrette asked. "Are we going to have a problem with that?"

Arlan shrugged. "We'll keep an eye on it, see what happens. But way I figure it, much as we're spending on this house, they better keep the water up or I'm gonna know the reason why."

For once I agreed with Arlan.

Despite Cheryl's protests, Arlan drove us all, with the exception of Cheryl, of course, who had to get some early morning rays, in the Land Rover into Cruz Bay where we rented two Suzukis — one with Willis's credit card, one with Larry's. Nadine and Lorrette were willing to ride around with whomever would take them, as long as they didn't have to pay.

Liz and I brightened up considerably on seeing Cruz Bay by daylight. It was a delightful little town of narrow streets, bustling tourist shops, and noisy bars and restaurants. Reggae music bounced off the cobblestone streets and battled with the sounds of laughter, boats, and cars. While the men attended to the manly business of renting cars, Liz, Nadine, Lorrette, and I wandered the narrow streets, sticking our heads in this shop or that shop, and looking into the open-air bars and restaurants.

We lost Nadine and Lorrette in a jewelry store. Liz and I kept going, finding a row of shops made out of little more than galvanized tin roofing and burlap. Inside we found arts and crafts made by residents of the island — colorful primitive-style paintings, shell sculptures, and coral sculptures.

To my chagrin, I ended up spending way too much money on a primitive-style painting of a schoolyard full of colorfully dressed children playing a game, with palm trees swaying behind them and the green mountain of the national park in the distance. It was already framed so I wasn't sure how I was going to hide this purchase from Willis. Even though I have my "own" money — my income from writing romance novels — Willis and I still tend to discuss any purchase over two hundred dollars. With tax, this purchase came to $197.50. I figured if I considered the shipping costs as another purchase entirely, then I was okay.

"We ship," the clerk confirmed. I smiled and gave her my mother-in-law's address, adding a note to let Vera know this was *my* painting, not something I was sending to her.

Which also made me think maybe I should buy her something nice while I was here.

Liz and I wandered out of the shop and found a sidewalk cafe where we ordered conch fritters and rum drinks. It was barely ten o'clock in the morning, but somehow drinking at that hour didn't seem the least bit weird. Not in paradise.

We weren't there long before Nadine and Lorrette found us. They ordered more fritters, and Liz and I ordered more drinks. By the time the men found us, the four of us were having a high old time, bonding like only four drunken women not used to drinking can bond.

We headed back to the car park, which was on the water's edge. As we started for our respective cars, Arlan pointed toward the dock. "Hey, there's Bud coming in!"

Sure enough, there he was — a new loud shirt, same old hat, a cigar sticking out of his mouth — bringing a dinghy into the dock. He got out and Arlan headed for him, but stopped.

"Aren't you going to say hi?" Nadine asked.

"He looks busy," Arlan said, and turned us all back around. Bud did look busy all right, and the beautiful young "darkie" woman he was busy with certainly wasn't Marge.

Nadine and Lorrette rode back to the house with Willis and me, all three of us yelling, "Stay left, Willis, stay left!" and giggling for all we were worth while he traversed the narrow, winding roads back to the house.

In daylight, the steep, downward driveway to the house was even more harrowing than it had been at night. And the house was even more beautiful. White stucco with blue tile roofs shone in the island sun.

To reach the parking area for the house, one had to come down the vertically challenging driveway, drive up practically to the front door, turn the car sharply, and try to back up to the flat cobblestoned surface that overlooked a huge bay rum tree, complete with hammock swing, and a grassy sweep of yard to the right of the deck and pool area.

Arlan was unloading groceries with Larry's help as we pulled up, so we grabbed some bags and went to the house, taking the rock stairway that passed our open-air shower to the side door of the kitchen area.

The grocery sacks contained several bottles of rum, assorted frozen cans and bottles of juice, an enormous amount of shrimp, and several bags of ice. There were a few real oranges, some bananas, some deli, but mostly more and more and more bottles of rum, largely the islands' own Cruzan.

In my present state of inebriation, the overstatement of rum seemed like a grand idea.

Unfortunately, I don't remember a lot about that first whole day on the island — there was the pool, a walk along the rocky beach, some frozen drinks, Jimmy Buffet singing about a cheeseburger in paradise over and over on the CD player, and more frozen drinks.

Later there was shrimp — lots and lots of shrimp — and more frozen drinks.

I slept well that night.

The next morning I awoke with a terrible headache that I knew only a warm shower would alleviate. I grabbed my robe and headed outside to the shower. Birds sang, boats creaked, and I figured I might live another day. I turned on the shower. Only a small dribble of water came out.

I went back into the bedroom and punched my husband none too gently on the arm.

"Shower won't work," I said.

He glared at me bleary-eyed. As I remembered it, Willis had pretty much kept pace with my frozen drink consumption.

"I don't care," he said slowly and distinctly.

I punched him again. "Fix it," I said.

"Tell Arlan, he's the head honcho around here." With that, Willis turned away from me and covered his head with the blanket.

I walked across the landing to the upstairs master suite and knocked on the door.

"Arlan?"

There was no answer so I knocked again. "Arlan!"

"Wha—" I heard from the other side of the

door. Finally, he opened it, leaning heavily against the door jamb. "What?" he said.

"The water's not working," I said.

From below us, Larry hollered up. "Hey, Arlan? We're not getting any water down here!"

"Who died and made me Gunga Din?" Arlan groused.

"This was your idea," I said, turned and headed back to my room where Willis was snoring soundly in bed.

I heard Arlan slam his bedroom door.

I sighed and got out of my pajamas and into some shorts and a T-shirt. Larry was just coming out of the downstairs master suite, also in fresh shorts and a T-shirt, when I came down the stairs. Liz was behind him, pulling a too-short blue silk kimono around her.

"How can we be out of water already?" she asked. "We seemed to have almost a full cistern yesterday."

Larry went to the trap door and I knelt down to help him lift it. The door was both heavy and awkward, but we got it up.

The water appeared to be even higher than the day before. So why weren't we getting any in the house? I reached down into the water to see if there was an impediment. It was then that I felt it. Which was about the same time as I started screaming.

I threw myself backwards across the living room floor; Larry was screaming, "Snake!" at the top of his lungs. Liz had run halfway up one of the stairways, only to get knocked back down by Willis running down with Nadine right behind him. Lorrette stood on the landing looking down, holding a terrycloth robe closed around her, and yelling, "What? What?" to no one in particular. Arlan flew down the opposite stairway, Cheryl not far behind him. He and Willis reached me simultaneously. Willis grabbed me, lifting me to a standing position, his arms around me. "Jesus, E.J., what is it?"

I pointed at the open maw of the cistern. "In there!" I breathed. "Something! In there!"

"Snake?" Arlan asked, looking past me to Larry, who had backed up to the door of the downstairs master suite.

"No," I said, shaking my head. "Something slithery, like hair or — I don't know! Oh, God!" I shuttered at the memory of the filmy, slimy mess touching my hand.

Willis looked at Arlan. "Seaweed?" he asked.

Arlan shrugged, looking at the cistern. "I don't know how," he said.

Willis let go of me and he and Arlan walked closer to the cistern, looking down into its dark, watery depths. Willis leaned down for a closer look. With his index finger, he pointed. "What's that?" he asked Arlan.

Arlan squatted next to Willis. "Heck if I know," he said.

The two men looked at each other, as if debating who would be the most macho. Finally

Willis sighed and lay down on the floor, his head and part of his chest over the open hole of the cistern. "Grab my feet," he said to Arlan, who did so.

Larry moved back into the living room, asking Arlan if he needed help. I moved closer, Nadine holding on to my arm.

Liz and Cheryl came down the stairs, Liz on the right, Cheryl on the left, with Lorrette following Liz some distance behind.

"I don't know, y'all," Lorrette said. "Maybe we should call the rental agent?"

"Naw, I got it," Willis said, his voice strained, as he reached into the water. "Pull me back!" he said.

Arlan and Larry grabbed a leg each and started hauling Willis backwards.

As they did so, the thing Willis was holding came partly out of the water. Willis saw it first, yelled, and dropped it. But he'd had it up long enough for others to see it. For me to see it.

My husband had been holding a human head in his hands, his fingers tangled around long, dark hair.

Willis jumped up and started rubbing his hands vigorously on his pajama bottoms. Liz was screaming, Larry was flailing his arms, and Lorrette was yelling, "What was it? What was it?"

Nadine, the registered nurse, took over. She pushed Arlan out of the way and grabbed Willis by the arm. "Get it out of there!"

To Liz, she said, "Call an ambulance! Now!"

Willis and Larry got down on the living room floor and dragged the body out of the cistern. It was a woman with hair in a long, dark, braided weave, wearing a long, white, gauzy dress, her dark skin showing through the sodden material.

Nadine turned the body over, brushing the hair from the face, looking as if she were readying herself to give CPR. But even I could tell there was no reason for that. The lips were blue, the eyes protruding, the neck purple with bruising.

Liz came running out of the kitchen where she had been using the phone. "Ambulance is on its way —" She stopped, looking at the body. Then she looked at her husband. "Uh, Larry?" she said.

Larry nodded. "I know," he said. "Weird."

"What?" Nadine demanded.

"Well," Larry said, the inappropriate smile firmly in place, "I think that's my new receptionist. Tracy." He nodded his head. "Yep, I'm pretty damned sure that's her."

Liz walked up and slapped her husband in the face. "Larry, how could you?" she cried, then ran for the downstairs master suite.

Cheryl turned to me. "Well, I hope you're satisfied!" she shrieked, a very unpretty look on her beautiful face.

"What?" I asked, looking around me for an explanation.

"This is all your fault! Mother told us all

about your penchant for finding dead bodies! But, my God, Eloise, we're on vacation!"

For the first time in my memory, my sister Nadine was nodding in agreement with Cheryl. Everyone, including Willis, seemed inclined to believe I had somehow brought this dead body in our midst.

"I didn't do it!" I wailed.

Willis put his arm around me. "We know that, honey," he said in that unctuous tone he gets that makes me want to rip off his head and tell God he died. "It just seems that where you go, dead bodies follow."

"Has anyone ever looked into your sister being a homicidal maniac?" I heard Lorrette whisper to Nadine.

I sighed. "Will someone please just call the police?"

The captain of police for Cruz Bay, Micha Robinson, showed up along with the ambulance. His skin was the color of mahogany, his hair military short, and his shoulders incredibly broad. He was a big man, both in height and weight, and he carried himself as if he were bigger still. He wore khaki shorts and a shirt with epaulets, knee-high socks, and brown wingtips, and carried a military-style hat with a lot of braiding on it in one hand. His voice had the beautiful island lilt to it that made his words seem almost palatable.

"Any of you know this woman?" he asked.

63

No one said anything, but all tried not to look at Larry. Finally, Larry said, "I think that's my receptionist from back home."

"Where is that?" Captain Robinson asked.

"Houston. Texas. In the States," Larry said.

The captain was nodding. "I know Texas," he said. "Been to the Alamo myself," he said, his smile showing beautifully even white teeth. "I like John Wayne," he said.

We all nodded.

"She come with you here to St. John?" the captain asked Larry.

Larry shook his head. "No, no, sir. I don't know what she's doing here. I barely knew her. I mean, she was new. Just started working for me less than a month ago."

"Um-hum," the captain said. "Your wife is with you here, sir?" he asked.

Larry pointed at the bedroom. "She's lying down," he said. "This was a shock."

"Your wife, she knows this woman?"

Larry nodded. Then shook his head. "Not knows like in, you know, knows, but she, well, she met her. Like just barely."

The captain looked at me. "Young lady," he said, smiling that great smile again, "you will go get the wife for me?"

I nodded. "Sure," I said. "You bet."

I went into the downstairs master bedroom. If it hadn't been for the horror of our earlier discovery, I might have been pissed at finally seeing the room we didn't get. It was gorgeous, but of course, I didn't really notice under the circumstances.

Liz was lying on the bigger-than-king-sized bed in the center of the room. "The police captain wants to see you," I said. "You okay?"

Liz had an arm over her eyes. "No," she said softly.

I sat down next to her on the bed. "Whatever you're thinking is probably wrong, Liz," I said. "Let's just wait and see how this works out."

She removed her arm and looked at me. "Are you trying to tell me you don't think my husband killed the bitch, or you don't think my husband was sleeping with the bitch?"

I shrugged. "Both. Either. Neither."

Liz sighed. "I hate this," she said, and got off the bed, following me into the living room.

The ambulance attendants were removing the body as we entered. Liz glanced at it quickly then turned away. Larry came up to put his arm around her, but she brushed it aside and went and sat down on the couch next to Nadine.

"You the Mrs.?" the captain said.

Liz nodded. "Elizabeth Standard," she said, holding out her hand to the captain, who took it and bowed ever so slightly over it.

"You know the deceased?" the captain asked.

"I've met her. She worked for my husband."

"And the rest of you," he asked, "any of you met the young lady before?"

Cheryl said, "I have. The last time I had my teeth cleaned."

Nadine held up her hand. "Me too. Last week. Larry had to look at this molar he crowned last year. I think I've got this crack in it —"

"Anyone else?"

Lorrette raised her hand. "I had some X-rays done a couple of weeks ago. I think I must have met her, but I don't remember."

The captain looked at Larry. "You do everybody's teeth?" he asked, smiling.

"We're family," Liz explained.

"Ah," the captain said. He looked at Willis and me. "You don't have any problems with your teeth?" he asked.

"We live in another town," Willis said.

"Ah," he said, then looked at Arlan.

"Larry's been after me for about a year now to come in, but for a man who deals with teeth for a living, I gotta say dentists scare the shit out of me," Arlan said and laughed.

"You are a dentist too?" the captain asked.

"No, no. I own some dental labs. Make dentures, you know, false teeth, that sorta thing." He slapped Larry on the back. "Dr. Standard here is one of my biggest clients."

The captain pointed a large finger at Arlan. "You gonna have to make you some false teeth for yourself if you don't go see the doctor here, huh?" he said and laughed. Arlan laughed. Larry laughed.

Willis grabbed my arm before I could step in and remind everyone that a dead, probably murdered, body had just been removed from the room.

"So, we all family, huh?" the captain said. "How so?" He looked at Liz for an explanation.

"We're sisters — the redheaded ones — all sisters," she said.

"And you and the doctor are husband and wife, and you," he said pointing at Arlan, "are married to?"

Arlan put his arm around Cheryl, who held out her hand to the captain, as if expecting it to be kissed. He bowed slightly over it. "And you two?" he said, pointing at Willis and me.

We nodded.

Then he looked at Nadine. "And you and your friend?"

"We're a couple," Nadine said, her head high, the expression on her face and her ramrod posture daring the captain to make something of it.

He raised an eyebrow, then grinned widely. "Lesbians?" he said. "How wonderful! I've never met lesbians!" He pumped their hands in a meaty grip. "We have the boys come here all the time, but I never met girls before! This is very exciting for me!"

Nadine and Lorrette exchanged a look. "Happy to oblige," Lorrette said.

He turned to Larry. "And you do her teeth like she's a member of the family, huh?" he said. He turned back to Lorrette. "Very nice. Your name?"

"Lorrette Carter."

He wrote everyone's names down in his book.

"Okay, now, Dr. Standard," he said, addressing Larry, "why do you think your receptionist comes to the island? Excuse me, Mrs., but was she your lover, Doctor?"

Larry emphatically shook his head. "Absolutely not! I have no idea why she's here!" He turned to Liz. "Honestly, honey," he said, his smile almost fading. "I barely knew the girl."

"The victim's name?" the captain asked.

"Ah, Tracy. Tracy —" He looked at Liz.

"Bishop," Liz supplied, not looking directly at her husband.

"Right. That's right. Bishop," Larry said, smile back in place. "Tracy Bishop."

"Ah. She was a beautiful girl, Doctor, I think?"

"Huh? Ah, well, I guess —"

"Larry, of course she was beautiful," Liz said. "For God's sake, don't make a complete ass of yourself."

"What?" Larry demanded. "I barely knew her! You know, Captain, the person you should talk to is Myra, my dental assistant. She was basically Tracy's supervisor. I had nothing to do with the girl. Myra's the one you should talk to. Surely Myra would know why she's not at work. I mean, why Tracy's here instead of in Houston where she belongs," he said, his voice trailing off into silence.

"Um-hum," the captain said, pen poised over his book again. "Myra's last name?"

"Slovak. Myra Slovak." Larry gave the captain the telephone number of his dental office.

"Okay, now," the captain said, smiling brightly. "You, lady," he said, then checked his book. "Mrs. Cheryl Hawker. You talk with the victim here on the island?"

Cheryl raised an eyebrow. "Of course not," she said. "I barely spoke to her at Larry's office."

The captain nodded his head. "Miss Lorrette?"

Lorrette shook her head. "Like I said, I don't even know that I saw her at Larry's office, except I probably did, what with her working there and me going in to see him. But I sure didn't see her around here."

"I did," I said.

All eyes turned toward me.

"Twice."

The captain looked at me. "Please, Mrs. Pugh. When was this?"

"Sunday night when we got in, I'm pretty sure I saw her at the boat dock. I ran over her foot with my rolling suitcase. At least I'm pretty sure it was her. And yesterday morning, very early, right at sunup, I *know* I saw her walking on the beach in front of the house. I waved at her, you know, just being friendly, but she didn't wave back. Actually, she just ran off when she noticed me."

"And you're sure it was the same young woman?"

"Positive," I said. "She was even wearing the same dress she had on when they pulled her out of the cistern."

"Very interesting," the captain said. "Anyone else see this young woman around here?"

Everyone shook their heads.

"This house I notice has an alarm system. Was it turned on last night?" Captain Robinson asked.

Arlan shook his head. "Too many of us wanted to sleep with our windows opened, Captain. You know, so we could listen to the Caribbean. So we decided not to turn on the alarm."

The captain pointed the beefy finger at us all in turn. "Not a good idea," he said. "This island is very safe, very safe, but you paying big money for this house, yes?"

We all agreed.

"That big money includes what I think is a state-of-the-art alarm system. You should use it." He smiled. "Then no more dead bodies in the cistern, huh?"

"Speaking of which," Cheryl said, "what *are* we going to do about the water? I'm certainly not drinking the water that's in there now!"

Every face turned to look at her, all slightly aghast.

Cheryl laughed. "Well, I don't care if you think that sounds crass, but I'm not!"

Yes, it sounded crass. But she also had a point.

FOUR

Captain Robinson left us around two that afternoon. He had taken a roll of pictures of the body before the ambulance personnel took it out, and he took another roll of the living room, the deck, the beach where I'd seen the young woman walking, and anything else that seemed to grab his fancy. Finally, he left us after jovially telling us not to leave the island anytime soon.

After he left, all eyes turned to Larry.

"What?" he said defensively. "I have no idea what she was doing here!"

"Tell me about her," I said, leading Larry to one of the couches.

"I don't know anything about her! Like I said, Myra dealt with her! I barely knew her."

"How old was she?" I asked.

Larry shrugged. "Early twenties?"

"Where was she from?"

Again he shrugged. "I haven't got the faintest idea."

"She was twenty-two," Liz said. "She was working full time and going to the University of

Houston extension program part time, studying accounting. Her mother lived in Galveston, which I understand is where she grew up."

"How do you know so much about her?" Nadine asked.

Liz glanced at Larry. "I make it my business to know these things," she said.

Larry jumped up from the couch, turning on his wife. All vestiges of his ever-present smile were gone. "That was over twenty years ago, Liz! For God's sake! Are you ever going to forget that?"

The look Liz gave her husband would have withered many a lesser man. "It doesn't appear so, does it?" she said.

"Twenty years ago," Larry said, addressing the rest of us, "I had a one-night stand with a girl who worked in the office I was sharing with another dentist —"

"I'd rather you didn't air our dirty laundry," Liz said.

"How can I not?" Larry demanded. "You've got them all suspecting I was having an affair with that — that — Tracy! Probably even suspecting I killed her! God, I didn't speak more than two words to her! Or any other woman for that matter!"

"Okay, Lar," Willis said, standing up and patting Larry on the arm. "Let's all calm down."

"Once, Willis! Once in twenty-three years of marriage! I know once is once too often, but Jesus, is she ever going to forgive me?"

"I forgave you twenty years ago, Larry," Liz said. "It's the forgetting I can't do."

Nadine patted Liz on the arm. "They're all scum, Lizzie," she said. "I've been telling you that for ages."

Cheryl yawned. "This is boring," she said. "Why don't you two take it in another room? I'm going to the pool."

I almost smiled. It was reassuring in a way to know that some things never changed — my sister Cheryl was the same self-absorbed bitch she'd always been.

"Mother says you have to drive me to the drugstore," I told Cheryl. I was fifteen, Cheryl sixteen, and she was the one with the driver's license.

"Why would I want to do that?" she asked, not looking at me as she perused the latest Cosmo *magazine while simultaneously painting her toenails.*

"I don't think it has anything to do with what you want, Cheryl," I said, as snippily as only a teenage girl can. "It's what Mother said to do."

Cheryl ignored me.

I kicked her, making her smear blood red fingernail polish on the flesh of her toe.

"God, you idiot!" she screamed. "Look what you made me do!"

"I need to go to the drugstore now!" I said.

"Don't tell me," she said, taking a Kleenex to her toe. "You have a hot date and you need a rubber, right?" She giggled.

"If that's all I needed, I'd just borrow one of yours," I said.

"Like some boy would want to screw you," she said, partly under her breath.

I kicked her again. She rolled over and grabbed my leg, knocking me to the ground. With my free leg I kicked her in the shoulder, then pushed her in the gut with the leg she was holding.

Cheryl hollered, let go, and jumped on me, straddling my chest. Grabbing handfuls of my hair, she started bashing my head against the, thankfully, carpeted living room floor.

Mother hollered from the kitchen. "Girls, behave! Don't you spill that nail polish, Cheryl, do you hear me?"

I got both feet under her stomach and shoved her off. She landed on her butt next to the couch. The spilled bottle of blood red polish was soaking quietly into the harvest gold shag carpet.

Cheryl sprang up and grabbed my head, shoving my face into the spilled polish. "Lick it up, turd!" she screamed.

Mother came out of the kitchen.

"Girls! Look at that mess! Cheryl, I've told you to be careful with that nail polish!"

"She did it!" Cheryl said, letting go of my neck.

I sat back, my face smeared with the mess from the floor.

Mother shook her head. "You girls play too rough," she said, bringing cleaning spray and a sponge into the living room. "Cheryl, take Eloise to the drugstore. She needs supplies."

"Supplies" was Mother's euphemism for sanitary pads. One didn't have a period, one had "her monthlies." One didn't buy pads, one "got supplies." Somehow, for Mother, this made it all a little bit cleaner. And I'm sure she figured my father had no idea what she was talking about.

"Clean your face, Eloise, you look silly," Mother said.

"Clean your face, Eloise!" Cheryl mimicked, sticking out her tongue.

I kicked at her, missed, and went upstairs to try to remove the nail polish from my face.

I could hear Cheryl honking the horn while I was still in the bathroom, trying to scrub the fingernail polish off my face. I did the best I could, then went downstairs and out to the driveway where Cheryl was behind the wheel of Mother's monstrous Oldsmobile, fuming.

She brightened up when she saw me. "Ha! Missed a spot!" she said. "Like your entire ear! Boy, do you look stupid!"

She laughed the entire time as she drove me to the drugstore, about five miles from our house.

Cheryl pulled into a parking spot, slamming on the brakes at the last minute. "Hurry up," she said. "I'm not waiting for you all day."

I got out and slammed the door as hard as I could and went in the store.

When I came out, Cheryl and the Oldsmobile were both gone.

I waited at the curb by the drugstore for an hour, then walked home. Cheryl was already there, sit-

ting on the floor redoing her toenails.

"You bitch!" I shouted when I came in.

She looked up, slightly startled. "Oh," she said, "it's you. What's your problem?"

"What's my problem? You left me at the drug-store! I waited an hour for you! Then I had to walk home! With the cramps!"

Cheryl shrugged and returned to her toes. "Oh, I ran into John Davies. We went for a ride."

I stomped for the stairs. "Well, I hope he knocked you up," I said.

He didn't, but somebody else did a year later.

My point being, Cheryl has always been totally self-absorbed, self-centered, selfish, and pretty much a Bitch with a capital "B." In case I haven't mentioned that.

There were lab technicians in the house that afternoon in a futile attempt to fingerprint the premises in hopes of coming up with something. Since this was a rent by the day, week, or month house, I figured they would find a lot of prints, and that none of them would do them any good.

The rental agent, a darkly tanned woman who could have been anywhere from thirty to fifty-five, showed up after Arlan's phone call. He introduced her to us.

Her name was Cindy and, after studying her for a moment, I put her closer to thirty than the upper range of fifty-five. Her skin, however, was certainly closer to the high end due to entirely

76

too much exposure to the ravages of the sun this close to the equator.

"Nothing like this has ever happened in one of my houses before!" she said, looking at us as if we'd brought this particular new rental problem with us.

"Well, I certainly hope not!" Liz said, taking the offensive. "We were led to believe that we were dealing with a reputable rental agency."

Cindy's eyes got big and her demeanor changed completely. "Oh, I assure you nothing like this has ever happened! I'm so sorry if you've been inconvenienced in any way. We'll get a truck out here immediately to replenish the water supply."

"Why don't you have them clean it before they add more water?" Liz asked pompously, raising one eyebrow and giving the rental agent her best "director of the group" look.

"Of course! That goes without saying —"

"I don't think so," Cheryl chirped in, always ready to play the bossy snob role. "We'd prefer you actually said it."

Cindy bristled, pulling herself up, her whole body tightening. "Of course. We'll have a cleaning crew out here immediately and, after the cistern is properly disinfected, we'll add fresh water."

Liz smiled lazily. "That's all we're asking," she said.

Cindy apologized three more times as she made her way up the stairs and out the front door.

Liz and Cheryl high-fived each other. "Fresh water's coming!" Liz said.

Fine, I thought. Meanwhile, I intended to bathe in the pool. Though even that thought made me wonder just how accustomed I *had* become to finding dead bodies. A young woman's life had been taken, the body left in my temporary home, and all I could think about was the water? Fine for Cheryl — that was about the level of her involvement with other human beings. Even Liz could be fairly self-absorbed. But I'd always thought better of myself. That at least I was more humanistic. That I cared about people. That that was the reason I so often got involved when someone I knew and cared about was killed or accused of killing someone else. But here I was, just like Cheryl, worrying more about clean water than a dead body.

It's because you're on vacation, I told myself. Myself answered. *So's Cheryl.* I told myself to shut up.

Leaving the lab techs to their tasks, we took all three cars and headed into Cruz Bay in search of an early dinner.

We went straight to Mongoose Junction, an open-air mall, where we found a large table in a patio restaurant. There we set about consuming conch fritters, boiled shrimp, raw tuna, and chips and salsa by the bucket load, all accompanied with several bottles of wine and a few dozen frozen rum drinks. So far, in two days on this trip I had consumed more alcohol than I had the entire previous year.

"So what do you think?" I asked Liz, who sat on my right, my husband on my left.

"About what?" she said, eyes downcast, not even the abuse of alcohol able to cheer her up.

"About this Tracy person," I said. "Why do you think she was here?"

Liz looked up at me. "I think she was screwing my husband and was jealous that he and I were coming to the island. So she followed him. They had a fight and Larry killed her. End of story."

I looked at my sister, my eyes big. "Do you really believe that?" I asked.

Liz shrugged. "Not really," she said. "But I intend to tell the captain exactly that!"

"Why?" I asked.

She looked at me again, her eyes blazing. "Because whether he killed her or not, I'm pretty damned sure he was screwing her! And I told him last time if he ever did it again, I would make him very, very sorry."

"So divorce him," I said. "Don't have him hauled in on a murder charge, for God's sake!"

She looked pensive. "Well, you know, he could have done it," she said. "He looks mild mannered and all, but let me tell you, the boy's got some depths you'd be surprised at."

"Okay, forget Larry for a moment," I said. "If not Larry, then who?"

Liz put down her fork and her drink and turned to me, giving me her full attention.

"That's just it, Eloise. He's the only one. She worked for him. She was beautiful. End of story."

I couldn't help but wonder what kind of relationship my sister and brother-in-law had that, after twenty-three years of marriage, she could so easily and readily accept him as the number-one murder suspect.

Larry was sitting on the other side of Liz. He leaned over and looked at us both. "Would you mind keeping your voices down?" he asked. "I don't think the people at the far end of the room know you suspect me of murder, but everybody else sure as hell does!"

"Larry, I don't suspect —" I started, but Liz was too quick for me.

"Then you shouldn't have invited your little tramp along on the trip, Larry. Try to remember to screw them in the office. Those are the rules. Not at our home, not on vacation. Got that?"

Larry threw up his hands. "That's it!" he said. He jumped up from the table. "I'm getting the hell out of here!"

He took off, leaving the restaurant and the rest of us behind.

"Liz, honey," Arlan said from across the table, "you need to lighten up."

"Fuck you, Arlan," she said, "and the horse you rode in on."

Liz too left the table.

I had always known this would be a fun vacation.

When we got to the parking area, Larry's Suzuki was gone, and Liz was nowhere to be seen.

"Maybe they're together," Nadine suggested.

"I guess we should keep an eye out for her on our way home," I suggested.

"Hey, y'all!" came a voice from the street. We all looked over. There were the Texans From Hell.

Bud came up and started pumping manly hands, while Marge finger-waved at the rest of us. "Saw some commotion at your place this mornin'," Bud said. "Y'all have a prowler?"

"No! A dead body!" Nadine said.

"Good Gawd almighty!" Marge said. "What happened?"

Between Arlan and Nadine, the story came out in detail, with "oohs" and "ahs" and "good Gawd, y'alls" coming from their audience.

"Well, seems to me a little nightlife is in order, don't you think, Arlan?" Bud said. "Gotta get your minds off that situation! Come on, y'all."

I pinched Willis on the butt and he responded, "I think E.J. and I will head back to the house."

"Yeah, okay," Arlan said. "And keep an eye out for Liz and Larry. I'm thinking Bud here's got the right idea! I wanna see me some Caribbean nightlife."

"That sounds like fun!" Lorrette said. "May we join you?"

Cheryl looked at Nadine, as she never looked directly at Lorrette. "As long as the two of you don't dance in public," she said. She turned and headed for the Land Rover, with Marge at her side, laughing a shrill laugh and beating Cheryl on the arm.

Lorrette held Nadine back as she lunged for our always diplomatic sister, and Willis and I headed for the remaining Suzuki. "House or with them?" I asked Nadine.

She sighed. "With them," she said. She waved. "See you later."

It was while we were driving home that it dawned on me I may have seen Tracy Bishop more than the two times I'd mentioned to Captain Robinson.

I was pretty sure she was the young woman who'd met Bud on the dock the day before.

When we got back to the house, without having found Liz or Larry, the sun was sinking over the horizon between the two strips of land that made Great Cruz Bay. Willis and I stood on the deck and watched it, the glorious colors changing the landscape, the water. He put his arms around me and I leaned against him, trying to pretend that we were alone — really alone — in this island paradise.

When the last ray had dipped into the waters of the Caribbean, Willis and I turned off the house lights and removed our clothes, heading naked into the lower end of the pool.

I'm not sure when the others got home that night. Willis and I were fast asleep by eleven.

We woke up the next morning to Nadine knocking on our bedroom door. "Have you seen Liz?" she asked, poking her head in our room.

"No," I said, leaning up on one elbow. "Why?"

"She's not here. Neither is Larry. And their bed hasn't been slept in."

I got out of bed. "Is their Suzuki still gone?" I asked.

"I don't know."

We walked through our room to the connecting bath, and from there to the outdoor shower where we could see the parking area. Only one Suzuki stood next to the Land Rover.

"Oh, Jesus, you think she's all right?" Nadine asked, panic in her voice.

"Yes, I'm sure they're together —"

"Maybe he killed her!" Nadine said, grabbing my arm. "It's not like he hasn't set a precedent!"

I rolled my eyes. "Nadine, for God's sake —"

"I think we should call the captain! Right now!"

"What about?" Willis asked, rubbing his eyes as he came up behind us.

Nadine turned on him. "Larry's killed Liz!" she said, grabbing his arm.

"Nadine!" I said, simultaneous with Willis's "What?"

"Liz and Larry didn't come home last night," I explained to my husband. "And I believe Nadine is overreacting."

Willis looked at the car park. "Damn. His Suzuki's not there."

"That's exactly what I'm saying!" Nadine said, her voice rising. "And their bed hasn't been slept in!"

"What's the matter?" Lorrette asked, coming out of the bathroom, tying her robe around her.

"Liz is dead!" Nadine wailed.

"No she isn't!" I said. "Nadine, calm down."

"What's all that commotion up there?" Arlan called from the bottom of the stone steps, down by the pool. He came up, dripping from a recent dip in the pool, wearing Speedos that no one built like Arlan should ever try to wear. His chest and back were so matted with wet hair it looked like he was still wearing clothes. Seminaked, with his long arms hanging by his sides and his short bow-legs nude, he looked even more like a toad — a toad standing on two legs.

"Have you see Larry or Liz?" I called down to him.

He shook his head, coming up the rest of the staircase. "Nope. They leave? Or not back yet?"

"Their bed hasn't been slept in!" Nadine said.

"Or they got up early and Liz made the bed," Arlan suggested.

"No!" Nadine said, shaking her head. "I can

tell! That bed has not been slept in!"

"You get under the covers and feel for body heat?" Arlan asked and chuckled.

Just then we heard the squeal of brakes as the second Suzuki made the turn onto the steep driveway.

"There he is!" Nadine shouted, pointing. "Is Liz with him?"

There were two people in the car; one could only hope the second one was Liz.

Larry maneuvered the car into the parking area and the two got out, Larry walking to Liz's side of the car to open her door. They held hands as they came toward us.

"Where have you been?" Nadine yelled. "I've been worried to death about you!"

Liz looked at her husband and blushed. Willis nudged me with his elbow and I suppressed a giggle.

Larry looked at Liz, his smile wider than usual, and much more meaningful. "We had some things to work out." He looked at the rest of us. "Hope we didn't worry y'all."

"Worry us?" Nadine said, throwing up her hands. "I was worried sick!"

"Yeah," Arlan said. "Ol' Nadine here figured you killed Liz while you were on your murder spree, Larry."

Liz's face got tight. "Larry didn't kill anyone! Nadine, don't be ridiculous." She turned to her husband and smiled. "I'm tired. Wanna go lay down for a while?"

He put his arm around her and they passed us, going down the steps to the deck and their room.

We all looked at each other. Lorrette and I giggled and Nadine rolled her eyes. "Heteros," she said under her breath as she headed back to her room.

After breakfast Willis and I took our Suzuki into Cruz Bay and rented snorkel gear. While there we also bought Vera a caftan that was way too sexy and I knew she'd never wear (but it was one size fits all and I figured I'd get it back next gift-giving time), the kids some T-shirts, and — please forgive me — a neckerchief for the dog that said MY PERSON WENT TO ST. JOHN AND ALL I GOT WAS THIS LOUSY SCARF.

We came back and got on our swimsuits and reef walkers and carried the snorkel gear out to the rock beach in front of the house. The last time I'd snorkeled was in Mexico back when Willis and I were very young and very stoned. I remember little about it.

But I think I'll remember the waters of St. John for the rest of my life. It was warm, like bath water just at the cooling stage, and so clear you could see the bottom way after you were no longer able to reach it with an extended toe. I put on the equipment and lay there in the water, the buoyancy of the Caribbean keeping me easily afloat, snorkel sticking out of the water, face and body immersed, and felt at peace for the first time in ages. Watching the peacock-colored fish, the coral, the strange and beautiful plants — but mostly, just doing absolutely nothing. Finding peace. The only sound was my own heartbeat.

I knew my next book check would be dedicated to a swimming pool in the backyard. But even in this peaceful place, the ravaged face of Tracy Bishop swam before me, fogging the colorful fish and plants. What had she been doing on the island? More to the point, what had she been doing in our house? Had Liz's initial suspicion of her husband been on target? Had Tracy Bishop followed Larry here? She *was* beautiful; I'd noticed that the first time I saw her, on the dock when we arrived, and walking in front of our house on the day of her death. But I'd seen her again on the day of her death, in the company of the Texan From Hell — Bud George. Did Larry know Bud before our day of arrival on the island? Interesting thought. And one I needed to look into.

I felt a hand on my shoulder and looked up. Willis was treading water beside me, the mouthpiece of his snorkel dangling so he could speak. "I saw a turtle over there. A big one! Come on, I'll show you."

"I don't want to go too far out," I said, still unsure of my sea legs.

"I'll be right beside you, honey," he said. "Trust me."

I tried not to remember what my father had

always said about anyone who used that phrase. "Don't eat at a restaurant called 'Mom's,' don't buy a car from a man wearing jewelry, and never trust anyone who says 'Trust me.'"

I decided to skip my father's advice and follow Willis further into Great Cruz Bay. I felt like Esther Williams with flippers. My stride was clean and smooth, my kicks a thing of beauty as I went deeper into the bay. Sticking my head under the water, I could see life that hadn't been in the shallower depths. Large, beautifully colored fish, strange-shaped things that moved and I could only assume were alive, and then the turtle.

Willis grabbed my arm and pointed and I saw it. It was bigger than me — must have out-weighed Willis by a hundred pounds. It was swimming away from us, and as far as we could tell, completely unaware of our existence. His strange little feet and arms battled the water, and he moved little more gracefully in water than on land. I say "he," but I must admit I never got close enough to know for sure — even if I had known how to tell for sure with a turtle.

When we came up, we were near the tip of land leading out to sea. I waved Willis toward shore and we headed closer in, taking the safer route back to our house — our house, shining white and blue in the morning light, the sun re- flecting off the surfaces of the two pools, bouncing off all the glass windows and tile surfaces. *Our* house. I wish.

We came out of the water, exchanging our flippers for reef walkers and headed up the path to the deck. Liz was sitting under the shade of the deck umbrella, a frosty drink in front of her, her long, knobby legs stuck out in the sun.

I sat down at the table beside her. "Well," I said, grinning, "looks like y'all made up last night."

Willis said, "I think I'll go clean up," and headed up the side staircase to our open-air shower.

Liz grinned back. "Yeah, we made up." She blushed and said, "And how!"

We both giggled.

"Seriously," she said, sobering, "I was way off base to be acting the way I was. Twenty years ago, when we'd only been married a short while and things weren't going all that well, Larry had a fling. We almost divorced over it, but we vowed to each other that nothing like that would ever happen again. I think I've been waiting all this time for the other shoe to drop. I know now that he's stuck by that vow. I believe him."

I reached over and hugged her. "Pretty neat being able to trust your husband, huh?" I said.

Liz frowned. "I think that's the problem. I don't think I really have trusted him since that incident over twenty years ago. I've been waiting all this time for it to happen again." She shook her head. "We talked a lot last night —

besides the sex, which was great," she said, grinning and shooting me a look. "But we talked more than anything else. I don't think either of us slept at all. I guess I didn't realize until last night how truly committed Larry is to me." She looked at me, a puzzled expression on her face. "It's like he's as committed to me as I am to him." She shrugged. "I guess I never really believed that."

"You do now?" I asked.

She nodded her head and smiled. "Amazing, huh? After all these years." She raised an eyebrow. "You trust Willis?"

I smiled. "Yep, I do. I know some women may think that's naive, but I know him better than anyone else in the world. And I also know he's not brave enough to run the risk of losing everything he's got."

She smiled back. "Point well taken," she said. "I think that just might be what kept Larry in line after that first time."

She looked behind her and whispered, "What about Arlan? You think he messes around?"

I shuddered. "Who'd want to?"

Liz giggled. "He's rich," she said.

"Which is what keeps Cheryl around for sure," I said.

Liz slapped me on the leg. "Hush, be nice."

"Don't try the mother routine on me, Liz. I'll have to gag."

"You know," she said, her face serious again, "you and Cheryl really need to work this out,

Eloise. It's been going on way too long. You're both adults now. Let bygones be bygones."

I shrugged. "We never have gotten along, Liz, you know that. I don't see how that's going to change."

She shook her head. "Wrong. Y'all got along fine until I went off to college. That's when all hell broke lose."

I shrugged again. "Whatever," I said.

We were all in the car, Mother and Daddy in the front seat, us girls in the back. I was eleven, and we were taking my big sister Liz off for her freshman year at college. We were driving from Houston to Austin, where Liz would be going to the University of Texas. I was very excited. I'd never been to a university before. It was a long drive and we stopped in the town of La Grange for lunch.

A very cute boy of about twelve or thirteen was sitting at the table next to ours with his parents. He looked our way several times, and each time he did, Cheryl would toss her hair and arch her back, trying to accentuate her newly developing breasts.

"Cheryl's got a boyfriend!" I sang, loud enough for our table and the one next to us to hear.

"Shut up!" Cheryl hissed at me.

I giggled. "If you don't stop flinging your hair, you're gonna get it in my burger!"

Cheryl glared at me then lowered her head to her plate without another word.

When it was time to leave I told Cheryl I had to go to the bathroom. "I'll be quick," I said, and headed for the restaurant's facilities.

I did my business, washed my hands, and went to open the door. It wouldn't budge. I pulled and pulled, then banged and banged, yelling "help" at the top of my lungs. No one came. The restaurant was very noisy, filled with travelers from Houston to Austin and vice versa.

I don't know how long I was in there, but finally a woman came to use the facility and opened the door. I was sitting on the floor crying.

"Honey! Are you okay?" she asked.

"I couldn't get out!" I cried.

"That's because somebody stuck a broom handle through the door! I'm calling the manager!"

The lady went in search of the manager and I crept out of the bathroom.

My family wasn't in the lobby of the restaurant waiting for me. Looking out the large plate-glass windows, I noted that our car was missing too.

They'd forgotten about me. They'd left me behind as if I never existed.

The manager found me sitting in the lobby, crying.

"Now how did that door get locked, young lady?" he asked me sternly.

I cried harder.

"Stop that, you hear?" He patted me ineffectually on the shoulder. "Hush. Where are your folks?"

I cried harder.

"Reba!" he hollered at one of the waitresses. "Come deal with this!"

An old woman who smelled strongly of tobacco

came and forced me to stand up. "Now, hush up, child," she said. "Stop the blubbering. Where are your folks?"

I pointed to the parking lot. "Car's gone," I managed to get out.

"Well, I never," the old woman said and walked up to the cashier. "Looks like her folks just done run off and left her!" she said.

"Poor little thing," the cashier said, looking at me. "Think we should call the po-lice?"

"Well, I dunno. Harry!" she yelled, bringing the manager back into the lobby. "Think we should call the po-lice?"

"What's she done?" Harry asked.

Reba rolled her eyes. "She ain't done nothing, Harry, but it looks like —" and here she turned her back on me and whispered, although I could still here her. "Looks like her folks done took off."

Harry looked at me and shook his head, making a "tsk, tsk" sound with his mouth. "Honey, you know what kinda car your daddy drives?" he asked me.

"Chevrolet," I said. "It's blue."

"Well," Harry said, looking at the tobacco-smelling old lady and the cashier, "guess we best call the highway patrol. See if they can stop 'em 'fore they get clean away."

Just then my father's big, blue Chevy pulled into the parking lot. I yelled and ran through the doors to the lot.

My mother jumped out of the car and hugged me. "Where did you run off to?" she said, in that

93

lovingly angry way only my mother could fully achieve.

"I got locked in the bathroom —"

"Oh, for heaven's sake," Mother said, and Daddy got out from behind the wheel.

"Now how did that happen, young lady?" he asked.

I looked in the back seat. Two of my sisters were looking at me, somewhat concerned. The only one who wasn't was Cheryl.

"Cheryl did it!" I screamed. "She locked me in there!"

Daddy opened the back seat door. "Cheryl, get out here now!" he said. Cheryl obliged. "Did you do that?"

"Do what?" Cheryl asked innocently.

"What makes you think the door was locked?" Daddy asked me.

The manager came out of the restaurant.

"This your little girl?" he asked.

"Yes, sir," Daddy said, face turning a little red. "Didn't count enough heads when we took off. Sorry about that. She give you any trouble?"

"No, sir," the manager said. " 'Cept the handle on the door to the Ladies is busted. Somebody stuck a broom handle in there and jammed it good. That's how come the little one here got stuck in there."

Mother and Daddy turned and looked at Cheryl.

"I didn't do anything!" she said.

"Cheryl Marie Henderson!" Mother yelled. "Tell the truth."

Cheryl hung her head.

Daddy brought out his checkbook. "How much I

*owe you for that door handle?" he asked the man-
ager.*

*The two men walked off to do a little dickering
and my mother took my arm and Cheryl's. "Now
you know you're both Mother's little angels. You
know that, now don't you?"*

*We both dutifully nodded our heads. "Now,
Cheryl, I want you to apologize to your baby sister
and I want you to hug each other's necks."*

*Cheryl mumbled, "Sorry," and reached for me.
We hugged. In my ear, she whispered, "I was
hoping they'd never find you."*

Lorrette came out with a drink and her pack
of cigarettes and sat down at the table.

I looked at the cigarettes longingly. It had
been almost thirteen years since I'd had one,
but sometimes the urge came back. Often
whenever I thought about my sister Cheryl.

"Beautiful day," Lorrette said, lighting up.

"I'm sure this could get boring after a while,"
Liz said, staring out at the bay and the boats.

"Yeah, personally I couldn't handle it for
more than thirty years," I said.

Liz pulled her legs in from the sun, poking the
skin to see how bad the damage was. "This is the
problem," she said, her fingers leaving semiper-
manent white spots where she touched the
scorched flesh. "You think wrapping myself head
to toe in Saran Wrap would help?" she asked.

I touched my shoulders where my fingers left
white marks from my fairly early morning time

95

in the water. "I doubt it," I said.

Lorrette laughed. "I used to envy Nadine all that great red hair, but now I'm rethinking it," she said, moving her chair into the sun and lifting her face to its rays. "Um," she said.

Liz and I said, "Bitch" in unison and all three of us laughed.

"Well, I'm going in and resting my poor skin," Liz said and followed the words with the deed.

I thought about going in, thought about getting a cool drink and bringing it back to the table, thought about a lot of things, but I didn't move. It was too wonderful sitting out there, listening to the chatter of the boat crews on the bay, to the tinkle and ping of the boats swaying in the water, the calls of birds, the hum of an inboard motor as one of the cabin cruisers in the bay hoisted anchor and made its way to sea; looking at the sun shine on the water, the brightly colored houses cling to the side of the hill, the greens, the blues, the bright pinks of the bougainvillea.

"Who's that?" Lorrette asked me.

I glanced where she pointed. In the grassy, shaded area beneath the car park, a man stood under the bay rum tree, one hand resting on the strap of the hammock swing.

He was tall, young, his skin coffee-colored, and his hair in dredlocks. He was wearing long, brightly colored cotton shorts and no shirt. He saw us looking and headed quickly to the rocky beach and away, his back to us as he strode purposefully down the beach.

"He wasn't supposed to be there, was he?" Lorrette asked.

I shrugged. "I don't think so. I think that's definitely part of this property." I watched the young man as he disappeared around a bend in the land. "Think we should tell someone?"

"Like the captain?" Lorrette asked.

I shrugged again. "Maybe."

"Um," she said.

We stared again out at the bay, seeing a cruise ship far off in the distance, beyond the land's end. Was it the sun, the water, the booze? Whatever it was, my curiosity wasn't the least bit piqued. Back home, with a murder victim in my living room one day and a strange man staring at the house the next day, I would have been alert — suspicious even.

But I was in paradise, and all that seemed to call for was tall, cool drinks and a good chair.

FIVE

After a few minutes Lorrette and I went to the kitchen and mixed up a batch of rum-raspberry coolers and took them out to the deck. The Land Rover was gone, Liz and Larry appeared to be "making up" some more in the downstairs master suite, and both Willis and Nadine were lying down in their rooms.

"I like Willis," Lorrette said out of nowhere.

"Huh?" I laughed. "Me too. Quite partial to him."

"Always makes a marriage work better," Lorrette said.

"May I ask you a question?"

She turned to me. "Shoot."

"How come you don't seem to male-bash like Nadine?" I asked.

She laughed and patted my arm. "Nadine's still fairly new at this, Eloise," she said. "She's still trying to justify her decision to let herself be who she is. It's easier to pretend that men are the enemy, that she had some rotten past with men."

"I always thought she and John got along fairly well." John was Nadine's ex-husband.

"They did," Lorrette said. "And she's beginning to be able to admit to that. She and John talk on the phone now about once a month or so, and she even laughs with him." She shrugged. "I think it's easier for him now that he's remarried. She's getting better, and I think she'll get better still."

"But you don't have those problems?"

She shook her head. "I knew I was attracted to women since I was in junior high," Lorrette said. "I tried dating in high school, but all the guys I went out with just turned into buddies." She laughed. "Hey, some of my best friends are men!"

I laughed.

"Seriously," she said, "I like men. I'm the only woman on my crew at work. When they first meet me, I'll admit, guys have one of two basic reactions to me: one, they're scandalized and a little repulsed, or two, it turns them on." She looked down at her hefty self in a bathing suit. "Even like this!" she said. "But usually the turned-on ones calm down pretty quick. The repulsed ones take a little longer — or sometimes not at all. That's one of the things I like about Willis. He doesn't fit either category. He just accepts me like I'm another human being. That's rare, you know." She laughed bitterly. "There's this one guy at work. We've worked together for eight years, and he's never spoken to me directly." She shrugged. "That bothers me some, but there are women who react to me

the same way. Your sister Cheryl, for instance —"

I made a rude sound and Lorrette laughed.

"Yeah, she's a pain in the butt for more reasons than that," Lorrette said. "But I don't
know, I guess I've gotten used to the way
people react to me."

"Hell, I get that same reaction from people
because I'm a liberal," I said.

She laughed. "They do seem to try to bunch
us all up together — pinko, liberal queers."

"Don't forget nigger-lovers," Arlan said,
coming around the side of the house.

Neither Lorrette nor I responded.

"Yep," he said, "pinko, liberal, queer, nigger-
loving tree huggers!" He laughed heartily at his
own wit, or lack thereof.

"Time to go in," I said, and headed inside.

The doorbell chimed as I moved through the
French doors into the living room. I headed up
the stairs, but Nadine came out of the room
above and opened the front door.

Although I couldn't see him, I recognized
Captain Micha Robinson's island lilt. I could
only pray he hadn't heard Arlan's disgusting remarks.

"I need to ask a few more questions," he said.
"Is everybody home?"

"Yes, sir," Nadine said. "Some are resting,
but —"

"Please, I hate to ask, but can you rouse
them?"

"Certainly," Nadine said.

I called up to her, "You get Willis and I'll get Liz and Larry."

I headed to the downstairs master suite and knocked on the door, hoping they were finished with whatever it was they had been doing.

"Liz?" I called, "Captain Robinson's here. He needs to talk to all of us."

I moved back into the living room and sat down next to Cheryl on one of the couches. She was checking her manicure, completely unaware of my existence.

Captain Robinson came down the stairs, followed by Nadine and Willis. The rest of us gathered in the living room.

"Dr. Standard," he said, smiling. "Ladies. Mr. Hawker. So sorry to bother you good people on your vacation, but what can I do?" he said, shrugging. "It is my job," he added sadly.

We all murmured our okays, and he went on. "Dr. Standard, I spoke earlier today with your assistant, Ms. Slovak, in Houston. Myra Slovak?"

"Yes," Larry said, nodding, the smile in place.

"She says the deceased, Tracy Bishop, did not come to work Monday morning like she was supposed to, and she didn't call in. She had no idea she was on the island."

"Well, neither did I!" Larry said, his voice defensive.

Captain Robinson patted the air with his hand. "I understand," he said. "I've been in

101

contact with a homicide detective in Houston, Detective David Pearson. You know him?" We all denied that we did. "He's going to check out Ms. Bishop's apartment and get back to me."

Larry nodded and smiled.

Captain Robinson looked at Liz. "You said Ms. Bishop came from Galveston?" he asked.

Liz said, "That was my understanding."

He nodded. "So was it Ms. Slovak's understanding. Do you happen to know her mother's name?"

Liz shook her head. Captain Robinson looked at Larry. Larry shook his head.

"Myra should have it on the application," Larry said. "Next of kin?"

Captain Robinson shook *his* head. "No. We checked. She left that part blank."

"Oh," Larry said.

Captain Robinson smiled broadly and clapped his hands once. "Well, that's it for now! I want to thank you kind people for putting up with me! The water, it's being taken care of?"

Arlan said, "Yep. Today. We got a truck coming in special."

The captain grinned and shook his great finger in Arlan's face. "Consider yourself privileged, sir! They don't do this for just anyone, you know!"

"Well, under the circumstances —" Arlan started.

The captain nodded his head. "Just so, just

so." He smiled. "I will leave you good people now. And again, I thank you for your time."

Willis walked Captain Robinson up the stairs and we all sighed in relief. That was over. For a little while.

By the time we got to Austin I was good and mad. I had been scared. Being locked in that bathroom had terrified me. I was eleven years old and equated being scared with being a sissy. My sister Cheryl had made me feel like a sissy.

We stayed at a motel near the university. We had two connecting rooms — a single for Mother and Daddy, and a double for us girls. Nadine and Liz had one bed, and Cheryl and I had the other.

Liz and Nadine talked Daddy into letting them have the car, and they took off to the wilds of the university — no doubt to try to pick up boys. Cheryl and I stayed home with Mother and Daddy, watching television in their room for a while, then heading to bed.

Neither of us said much to each other that night. There didn't seem to be a lot to say.

I woke up around midnight. The bed where Liz and Nadine should have been was still empty and the light was still on under the connecting door to Mother and Daddy's room.

Cheryl lay beside me, sleeping soundly, her long, strawberry blond hair flared out behind her on the pillow, long lashes resting against her peaches and cream cheeks.

I crept out of bed and opened my overnight bag.

My Aunt Rosie had sent me a manicure set for my birthday and I'd brought it along, on the off chance that I might do my nails — something I had as yet been uninspired to do, but it was a neat case and I thought it looked grown-up to pack it.

I opened the case and took out the manicure scissors. I'd used them only once, to cut the string on some tin can telephones my friend Mike and I made.

I crawled back into bed and sat there, looking down on my sister. At all that strawberry blond hair cascading behind her.

I bent over and very carefully began snipping the hair, getting as close to the scalp as I could. I cut and cut and cut, reaching all that I could with the way she was lying there, then I carefully got back up and put the scissors back in their case and the case back in my overnight bag.

I lay back down on the bed, a smile on my face, and went to sleep.

The next morning I awoke to Cheryl's screams. Screams that didn't seem to ever want to stop.

I looked out the window of our room, staring down at the boats anchored in Great Cruz Bay, and remembered those screams. Remembered the hair everywhere. Remembered the little stubs and fluffs of hair left on Cheryl's head, and the great strands of hair in the back where I hadn't been able to reach.

Everyone had stared at me that morning, shocked speechless. Then my father walked up to me and slapped my face.

I was stunned. Daddy had never touched me — ever. Not ever in my entire life. And here he went and slapped my face.

Mother looked at him, also stunned. But she didn't do anything. She didn't say, "Henry, how could you?" Or, "My God, what did you do to my little angel?"

She didn't say anything. The only sound was coming from Cheryl — a high keening as the loose strands of hair played through her fingers.

I remembered it all as if it were yesterday.

Liz had been right. Cheryl and I had gotten along okay until that weekend Liz went off to college. But Cheryl had done something bad, and I had done something worse.

When we got back home, Mother bought Cheryl a wig which she wore until her hair grew out. Neither incident was ever spoken of again. Except for the slap in the face, I was never punished for what I did, nor was Cheryl. After Cheryl's hair grew out enough for the wig to come off, the incident was totally behind us, and it became THAT BIG THING THAT NO ONE EVER TALKED ABOUT.

And it had never healed. Not in twenty-eight years.

I went downstairs and found Cheryl sitting on one of the couches in the living room, a beauty magazine in her hand. Her beautiful hair was pulled back in a high ponytail, and she wore dark blue shorts with a matching top, long limbs smooth and silky, nary a freckle or wrinkle in sight. She looked up when I entered the room, her blue eyes shining at me.

"Well, Eloise," she said. "Having fun?"

I smiled weakly. "A blast," I said.

I went into the kitchen and grabbed my husband. "Let's go for a drive," I said, and headed out of the house.

We drove up the mountain, into the center of the island. The roads were narrow and twisty, and the speed limit was a generous twenty miles an hour. I felt as though Willis was speeding recklessly when he made it to fifteen. Often one side of the road clung precariously to the side of a steep hill, trees and shrubs growing to the very edge of the tarmac, while the other side dropped off to the Caribbean, often a hundred feet below. The views were spectacular, if you could manage to keep your lunch down. The going was made even slower by the cows, horses, pigs, chickens, and occasional mongoose that meandered across the road.

About an hour later we reached the little hamlet of Calabash Boom. All I could see were a couple of shops, some houses, and an open-air cafe. We pulled the Suzuki to the side of the road where there was a narrow strip to park, and went to the cafe. We ordered conch fritters, shrimp salads, and rum.

"What's wrong?" Willis asked me.

"Wrong?"

"Don't start," he said. "You've barely said a word all the way here. Tell me."

So I told him. About being trapped in the bathroom. And about my revenge.

When I finished his eyes were big. "*You* did that?"

I nodded. "Pretty awful, huh?"

He blew air out of his mouth, turning his head so that he wasn't looking at me. Finally he turned back. "Doesn't seem like something you'd do."

I nodded. "I know." I felt tears sting my eyes. "It was the worst thing I've ever done in my life."

"Jesus, honey, you were eleven years old! Lighten up on yourself!"

"Our girls are ten. What if Megan were to do that to Bessie now? At age ten? What would you think?"

He looked away from me again. "I guess I'd think maybe a couple of extra years with our family therapist."

"Exactly," I said. "It wasn't a rational thing to do." I sighed. "And my daddy slapped my face."

Willis looked at me. "He slapped you?"

I nodded. I couldn't say anything. After all these years, I could still feel the sting of tears behind my eyes.

Willis touched my hand. "Honey, that was a long time ago."

"Yes," I said, my voice barely above a whisper.

"Coming here wasn't a good idea, was it?" Willis asked.

I looked around the open-air bar. "What's wrong with it?" I asked.

"Not here here," he said. "Here St. John. With all of them."

I shrugged. "I don't know," I said. "I'm not sure if agreeing to come here was the worst idea I've ever had, or the best."

"Not to mention another dead body," he said, gallantly changing the subject.

"Oh, I almost forgot." I told him about the young man Lorrette and I had seen standing under the bay rum tree beneath the car park.

He frowned. "Why didn't you say something right then?" he demanded.

"Lazy," I said and grinned. "There's something about this island."

He grinned back. "I know. I almost didn't floss this morning."

"Whoa, watch out," I teased. "Next thing you know you'll be letting your nose hairs grow."

"Seriously, why didn't you tell Captain Robinson about this?"

"We thought about it when it happened," I said, "but I think we both just forgot."

Willis took a long drink of rum. "When we get back we'll call him."

"Okay," I said, signaling the waiter for another one.

We left Calabash Boom and kept going west, away from Cruz Bay, until we reached the far side of the island. The sun was beginning to set and we found a sand beach and walked along it, arm in arm, dipping our toes in the warm Caribbean, and watching the colors of the sky and sea multiply, divide, and disappear.

There was a party going on when we got back to the house. Bob Marley was confessing to having shot the sheriff — but again denied that entire business with the deputy — while Liz and Larry danced on the deck. The Georges were back with us, and they appeared to be attempting to dance as well. Bud had lost his sandals somewhere, but his socks were still firmly in place as he slipped and slid around the deck, arms flailing in yet another loud tropical shirt, while Marge's bottom was a sight to behold bouncing around the deck clad in skin-tight polyester. If I'd had a video camera and a penchant for blackmail, I could have been a wealthy woman.

Nadine was laughing excessively at something Arlan was saying, while he poured her what I'm sure wasn't her first drink from what I'd swear wasn't the first batch of frozen rum concoctions of the evening. Cheryl and Lorrette were hunched across the table on the deck, both talking at the same time. And to each other. Ah, the miracle of booze.

Arlan saw us and held out the pitcher of drinks. "Y'all gotta catch up!" he said. "Come on, grab a glass!" He searched the table for an empty glass. "Oops," he said. "Here!" He thrust the pitcher at Willis. "Just drink it straight from here!"

Nadine thought that was the funniest thing she'd ever heard.

I went in the kitchen and got Willis and me glasses and poured us drinks. Then the two of us sat down and watched the show, in that superior way only the sober can watch the drunk.

It was the next day before I even thought about calling Captain Robinson.

It was raining, and the thought of being cooped up with my sisters and their spouses, even in that beautiful house, was a little too much for me. I suggested Willis drive me into Cruz Bay. I was still too much of a coward to attempt left-lane driving, besides which, the car had been rented in Willis's name and I wasn't on the list to drive it. Which was quite all right by me.

We volunteered to take the garbage with us and headed out before breakfast, dumping our refuse at the community Dumpster after sitting in a line of cars for about fifteen minutes for the pleasure of doing so.

Even the storm clouds on that island paradise were more exotic than back home. The dark grays were deeper, filled with danger, and the darkness of the sky only seemed to make the turquoise of the sea more brilliant. Palm fronds swayed in the heavy breeze and the sharp colors of the bougainvillea contrasted brilliantly against the dark sky, the rain on the petals sparkling like diamonds.

We got to Cruz Bay and hunted down breakfast first, which we found in a small sidewalk cafe near the police quarters. We sat under an umbrella, eating fruit and pastries and drinking dark, strong coffee, while the rain beat a tattoo on the canvas. The reggae music had already started in the shops and bars, and the sounds of the rain, the music, the hiss of tires on wet pavement, and the lonely sounds of boat horns bleating in the distance mixed together in a symphony of sound like nothing I'd heard before. Exotic. Paradise. And some day soon I would have to leave.

We left the cafe and headed to the office to find Captain Robinson.

He was there, in the outer office, sitting at a desk and talking on the telephone. I really couldn't understand anything he was saying — his speech was rapid-fire in a heavy patois, making it difficult for American ears to understand. He saw us and waved us to a seat.

When he got off the phone, he grinned widely at us. "Welcome," he said, spreading his arms wide. "What brings you to my neck of the woods?"

"Well, I forgot to tell you something yesterday when you were at the house," I said.

He frowned and cocked his head. "Oh? And what was that?"

"Well, I guess maybe an hour or so before

you got to the house, I was sitting outside with my sister Nadine's friend —"

"Ms. Carter?" he asked.

"Lorrette Carter, yes," I said, nodding. "Anyway, we were talking, not doing much of anything really, when she noticed someone standing on that little stretch of lawn beneath the car park?"

He nodded, letting me know he understood where I meant.

"Anyway, it was a man. A black man. Young. Maybe early to mid-twenties. Hair in dredlocks. I really can't describe his features — he was standing in the shade. But he wasn't wearing a shirt and he had on bright orange flowered shorts."

"Um-hum," the captain said.

There was a silence.

Finally he leaned forward. "That's all?" he asked.

I nodded. "Yes. When we looked at him he left, going in the opposite direction, so I never got a good look at his face."

"Did Ms. Carter?" he asked.

I shrugged. "I don't know. We really didn't discuss it."

"Had you seen this young man before?" he asked.

I shook my head. "No, that was the first I'd seen of him."

"And you don't think you would recognize him again?"

112

I frowned. "Probably not. I'm sorry."

He stood up and smiled. "Thank you for bringing this to my attention, Mrs. Pugh. Mr. Pugh."

He showed us to the door and we left.

Once outside, Willis and I looked at each other. Willis shrugged. "Well, we did what we were supposed to do," he said.

"I suppose so," I said.

The rain had stopped, leaving everything sparkling clean, the smell of wet earth and grasses tickling our noses. We were headed down the steps when we heard the honk of a horn.

Looking out at the street, we saw the Georges waving frantically at us from a rented Suzuki.

"Hey, y'all!" Marge called out. "What are you doing out and about this early?"

We reluctantly walked up to the car. "Hi, Marge," I said. "Bud."

"You been in the po-lice station?" Bud asked. "Talking about the body and all?"

"We had some information for the captain," I said.

Bud laughed. "Captain! Ain't that a grand name for a little hick nigger cop."

I'd had it. "I don't appreciate that kind of language, Bud," I said. "And I don't think the captain deserves your disrespect. Excuse me."

I turned and walked away.

Behind me I could hear Marge saying, "Well, what we say? I never! Bud, what we say?"

Willis caught up with me and we headed for Mongoose Junction, the shopping area where we'd eaten dinner the night before. It was new and pricey, but it was a beautiful area, the buildings made of Caribbean stone with shaded terraces and lush tropical plants surrounding dozens of shops and galleries.

As we walked up the steps to the first store, we heard behind us, "Now, y'all just hold up there a darn minute!"

We turned. Bud and Marge were hurrying towards us. "Little lady, I just want to apologize a whole hell of a lot for offending you back there," he said. "Didn't mean nothing by it. Just ole talk, you know? Way I was raised, sad to say. Our boys are after me all the time to cut out that kinda talk. But you know, old dog, new tricks!" He laughed heartily. "Forgive me, darlin'?" he asked, taking my hand in his.

"Really, Eloise," Marge said, grabbing my other arm. "He's just an old pistol! He don't mean to talk that way! Why, some of our best friends is negroes."

"Really?" Willis asked.

"Why yes! My friend Leticia comes over to my house once or twice a week, don't she, Bud, and she's just as black as the ace of spades!"

"Cleans good, does she?" I asked.

"Best housekeeper I ever had!"

But the thought struck me just then that there was something else I had neglected to tell the captain — mainly the thought that I had

114

seen the victim a third time, in the presence of Bud George. I wondered what Marge would think if she knew how closely engrossed Bud had been with the beautiful, young, and very black woman.

I suppressed a giggle, trying to remind myself that I wasn't near as big a bitch as I often wanted to be. I felt a pinch on the back of my arm and turned to see Willis looking at me sternly.

"Everyone has a right to their opinions, Bud," Willis said. "But we also have the right not to want your opinions thrust in our faces. Is that fair?"

"Oh, golly, yes!" Marge said. "Just as fair as fair can be. Right, Bud, honey?"

"Damn straight! And it's right white of you to take that attitude," Bud said with a straight face.

I felt the pinch again as I started to say something and shut my mouth.

Willis smiled. "Well, that's great," he said. "And it was nice running into y'all. Now we've got to go pick up some trinkets for our kids." He led me away, his hand firmly on my arm, while my elbow blasted away at his ribs. We were three stores away before we both burst into hysterical laughter.

Okay, I love to shop. There's nothing inherently evil in that. Not really. I don't spend loads of money on fancy clothes, I don't have an entire closet dedicated to shoes, and my jewelry consists mostly of my wedding ring and a strand of pearls inherited from a great aunt.

I like stuff. Bookends, wall hangings, tacky souvenirs, T-shirts, books, little boxes, exotic coffees, and chocolates I've never had before. To me, that's shopping. Finding the little hidden treasures and paying as little for them as possible. Now, that's heaven.

Willis and I wandered the shops, finding a trinket here, a treasure there, something hideously tacky someplace else. We spent less than fifty dollars and drove back to the house loaded with shopping bags. Now all we had to do was get this stuff home on the various airplanes.

When we got back to the house there was an extra Suzuki in the driveway. Willis and I looked at each other. "Bud and Marge," we said in unison.

Willis looked longingly at the driveway behind us. "Can't," I said, reading his mind and body language. "Have to face the music."

He sighed and parked the car. As we got out I caught movement out of the corner of my eye from the top of the driveway, high above us. I turned.

There he was again. This time he was wearing a shirt and I could see his features clearly in the morning light. But by the hair and the stance, I knew it was the same guy.

"Willis," I said quietly, hoping the man hadn't noticed me noticing him. "It's him."

Willis jerked around.

"Damnit!" I hissed. "Be discreet!"

Willis saw the young man and went charging up the driveway. Discreet, my ass.

The other man took off running, and by the time Willis reached the top of the steep incline, he was nowhere to be seen.

Coming back down to where I stood by the car, still breathing heavily from his run up the driveway, Willis said, "That was him? You sure?"

He bent his knees, leaning over and resting his outstretched arms on them, trying to catch his breath.

"Oh, yeah," I said. "That was him."

"Let's go inside," Willis said. "Call the captain."

SIX

I was five and Cheryl was six. We lay on a blanket in the grass, staring up at the sky as it lit up with fireworks. Nadine and Liz had wandered off, probably looking for boys, and Mother and Daddy were talking to another couple several feet away.

Cheryl and I stared up at the brightly lit sky, marveling at the wonders of pyrotechnology.

"Wow," Cheryl said.

"Wow," I repeated.

"Cool," Cheryl said.

"Cool," I repeated.

Cheryl giggled. "Don't copy me!"

"Don't copy me!"

She hit me in the arm. "Stop it!"

I hit her back and giggled. "Stop it!" I said.

A big boy came running by our blanket and hit my leg, tripping slightly and running on. I cried out with alarm.

"Hey!" Cheryl yelled at the boy. "You hurt her! You creep!"

She leaned over me. "You okay?" she asked.

I sniffed, wiped my nose on my arm, and nodded my head. "He scared me."

She put her arm around me. "He was just a big idiot! Nothing to be scared of! I'm here," she said. "I'll always protect you."

It hit me like a lead balloon. A good memory of my sister. I shook my head. Naw, couldn't be. There weren't any of those.

I checked my memory, worrying it like a sore tooth. Is that what happened? Am I really remembering this, or just wishing it?

I looked at Cheryl sitting across the patio table from me, cool drink in hand as the dying rays of the sun cast their spell on the sky and all who watched. Cheryl sitting there like a stone goddess, cool and untouchable, unfeeling, uncaring, utterly unreachable.

We sat there with our arms around each other until Mother and Daddy came back. "Oh, look at that!" Mother exclaimed to Daddy. "My little angels!"

Cheryl pushed me away then. And I wanted to go.

"What are you staring at?" Cheryl asked me, taking a sip of her rum concoction.

I smiled. "Nothing," I said. "Just remembered something pleasant."

One beautifully arched eyebrow rose. "Not about the two of us, I hope? There can't be any of those!" She laughed.

I laughed, too. "That's what I thought, too," I said, then I got up and went into the kitchen. It was time for more rum.

Willis had called the captain about our second visit by the dreadlocked stalker as soon as we'd gotten in the house earlier. He hadn't seemed overly impressed. He'd asked Willis if the man was still there; when Willis reported he'd run off, the captain had basically blown Willis off. I supposed he would have been happier had we hog-tied the young man and presented him to the captain decorated with a ribbon. Unfortunately, Willis hadn't been fast enough for that.

Later that evening, Willis and I called the kids at Vera's house.

"How's everything going?" I asked Vera.

"Just fine. These kids never misbehave around me, you know," she said, in that way she has of driving me crazy. "I think you let them get away with too much, that's your problem."

"I'm so glad you were finally able to solve *my problem*," I said.

"Well, one of 'em anyway," my mother-in-law said and laughed.

"May we talk to the kids?" I asked.

"Just hold your water. Y'all having fun? Tell me about the island!"

"It's beautiful," I said. "A real paradise. And the house is gorgeous! I'll bring pictures home."

"Don't tell her about the body!" Willis mouthed.

I nodded. "Went snorkeling, shopping, driving around the island. It's great," I said.

"Let me talk to her," Willis said. Taking the phone from me he said, "Hey, Mama. How're the kids? . . . Uh huh . . . Really? . . . Uh-huh . . . Okay." He grinned. "Hey, sweet pea, how you doing?" He mouthed Megan's name.

I grabbed the phone. "Hi, honey!" I said.

"Mom, you won't believe what's been going on at school! You know Rachel Rodriguez? Well, let me tell you what she did — hey!"

"Mom?" Graham's voice. "Shut up!" he said, presumably to his sister. "Listen, you didn't leave us enough money. Grandma won't even let us get a pizza! Send us some money!"

"Mama?" Bessie's voice. "Go away! Mama, when are you coming home?"

"Soon, sweetheart," I said. "Are you having a good time with all the animals?"

Bessie sighed. "I suppose so," she said. "But this is getting old, Mother."

Willis took the phone from me. "Bessie, baby, it's Daddy . . . Uh-huh . . . Soon . . . Yes, Sweetie, I miss you, too . . . Uh-huh . . . Let me talk to Graham . . . Son, you taking care of your sisters? . . . We left you fifty dollars . . . You can't have spent it all already . . . Let me talk to your grandmother . . ."

And so it goes.

The doorbell rang very early the next morning. Rum, early mornings, and ringing bells are not a good combination. I staggered out of bed, grabbed my robe, managed to get it on backwards, and rushed to the front door, hoping against hope to stop the blasted pealing of the bell.

I threw the door open and stared out at Captain Micha Robinson.

"What?" I demanded, none too graciously.

"Good morning, Mrs. Pugh," he said, smiling that 1,000-watt smile. I wished I'd remembered to put on my sunglasses before opening the door. "May I speak to Ms. Carter?"

"She's asleep," I said. "Everybody's asleep. I *was* asleep. We're on vacation, you know," I said, my tone undoubtedly accusatory.

"So sorry," he said, "but it is important that I speak with her. Privately," he said.

At this point I noticed that his face was very serious. The smile was long gone.

I held up my hand, indicating that he wait, while I turned and knocked on the door of the smallest bedroom. "Lorrette?" I said. "You awake?"

She came to the door bleary-eyed. "What?" she said, not the least bit happy with me.

"Captain Robinson needs to talk to you," I said.

"Me?" She looked past me at the open door. "What for?" she whispered.

"I don't know," I whispered back. "He said *privately.*"

Lorrette looked at me, at the open door, and back at me. "Shit," she said.

I nodded my head.

"Just a minute."

She closed the door to her bedroom and a second later opened it, pulling a robe around her.

She went to the open doorway, with me close behind her. "Captain," she said.

He smiled slightly. "Ms. Carter. May I speak to you a moment please? In private," he added, giving me a look.

Lorrette turned and looked at me, then slipped through the front door, closing it behind her. From the window next to the door I could see them walking toward the car park.

The small bedroom door opened and Nadine stuck her head out. "What's going on?"

My bedroom door opened and Willis came out, pajama bottoms and no top, scratching his belly and stretching. "What's all the commotion?"

Slowly, bedroom doors opened and we all gathered in the living room. Willis went in the kitchen to start coffee, while I told the rest what had happened.

We all looked up at the silent and steadfastly closed double doors on the floor above.

"Why does he want to talk to Lorrette?" Nadine demanded. "She didn't even remember meeting that woman!"

Cheryl yawned prettily and smiled at Nadine. "Think she's been stepping out on you?"

Arlan moved Cheryl behind him while I

grabbed Nadine. "Cool it," I said in her ear. "She's trying to provoke you."

"Whose idea was this stupid trip?" Nadine demanded.

The door finally opened and Lorrette came through it. "Lorrette," Nadine called, but Lorrette turned and went into their bedroom, ignoring all of us.

Nadine looked at me, her face grim, and headed up the stairs to be with her partner.

The rest of us went into the kitchen where the smell of coffee was calling us.

We fixed a quick breakfast. Nadine and Lorrette did not join us.

We decided on a snorkeling excursion to Cinnamon Bay Beach and, gathering up the equipment, went up the stairs to the front door.

"Let me check on Nadine and Lorrette," I told Willis. "I'll be right with you."

I knocked on their door. After a long moment, Nadine opened it a crack. "Oh, good, it's you," she said, then grabbed my arm and pulled me inside.

"We're headed for Cinnamon Bay to go snorkeling. Y'all want to join us?" I asked. One look at Lorrette told me the answer to that question.

Her eyes were red and puffy and the ashtray on the bedside table was heaping full of used butts.

"You have to help us, Eloise," Nadine said. "Mother told us both about all your snooping and stuff. All the murder business you've been

124

involved in. You have to help us."

"What's going on?" I asked.

Nadine sat me down on the bed, then took a seat next to me. "Lorrette," she pleaded. "Tell her."

Lorrette sighed, took a deep breath. "The captain seems to think I'm implicated in that girl's death. That Tracy person." She looked at me, her eyes beseeching me. "God, Eloise, I never even met her! I swear to God!"

"Why would he think you're implicated?" I asked, genuinely confused.

There was a knock on the door. Nadine jumped up, shushing us. She opened the door a slit, then turned to me. "It's Willis," she whispered.

I walked to the door. "Could you tell the others you and I'll catch up with them later? Something's come up."

He gave me a searching look, then nodded his head. God, I married a good man.

I closed the door and went back to the bed.

"Why?" I repeated.

Lorrette looked at Nadine, who nodded her head. Again Lorrette sighed. "I used to live in Galveston. For ten years. I taught high school there." She ground out the cigarette she'd been smoking and lit a new one. "I was a good teacher," she said emphatically, defensively. "A really good teacher. The kids even voted me teacher of the year for 1989." She smiled weakly. "That was a very big deal for me."

I touched her hand. "Galveston," I said. "That's where Liz said Tracy Bishop was from."

Lorrette nodded her head. "Yeah. Actually, she could have gone to that high school during the years I taught. But I don't remember her. I don't remember the name and I don't remember the face."

"Well, for God's sake! How does the fact that you taught in Galveston implicate you in this girl's death?" I demanded. "I thought the captain had some brains! This is ridiculous."

Nadine sighed. "Tell her, honey," she said.

"I was living with another woman then. Her name was Barbara. She was a student at the medical school there in Galveston. We were discreet. We had a two-bedroom, said we were roommates. You know the drill."

I nodded my head.

"But I had this student," Lorrette went on, "a girl named Candy. She was an under-achiever. Smart kid, but refused to apply herself to anything except boys and booze. And maybe smoking dope, who knows? I was on her case a lot. I knew she could make more of herself. She was smart. Really smart." Lorrette laughed. "Too smart for me, it turns out." She sighed. "Somehow she found out about Barbara and me. Maybe she saw us in an indiscreet moment — I don't know. But I threatened to flunk her that semester because she wasn't doing her work. So she threatened me. She said if I flunked her she'd tell the principal I was a dyke. Her words. Said she knew I was and she'd tell." Lorrette shrugged. "I thought, fine. Let her tell. I had tenure. Hell, I could even deny it if I wanted to. So I flunked her."

Nadine moved and went to sit next to Lorrette, putting her arm around her "Did she tell the principal?" I asked.

Lorrette laughed bitterly. "Oh, yeah. She told. She not only told the principal I was a lesbian, she told him that I seduced her and that she and I had been having a lurid affair the entire semester. And that when she tried to break it off, I flunked her."

"Oh, God," was all I could think to say.

"I was brought up on charges." She shook her head. "I don't think the kid wanted it to go that far. She just wanted to get back at me, and not flunk the course. But the principal told her mother and her mother called the police and the next thing I know I'm hauled up on charges of statutory rape, indecency with a minor, and that good old Texas standby, sodomy. Barbara's called in at the medical school, implicated by the mother for some reason . . ." Lorrette took a long drag on her cigarette. "The long and short of it was the charges were finally dropped. But not before I lost my job, and not before my relationship with Barbara was totally ruined. I left Galveston, left Barbara, and left teaching."

"And this is what Captain Robinson thinks implicates you?" I demanded.

"Where there's smoke —" Nadine said.

Lorrette laughed. "There's a smoking lesbian," she said, exhaling a cloud of cigarette smoke.

"How in the world did he find this out?" I asked.

Lorrette shrugged. "I'm sure he did checks on all of us. I'm the lucky one with a criminal record, which just happened to be from the same city where Tracy Bishop supposedly grew up."

"Are we even sure about that? Is he taking Liz's recollection on this? I mean, she could remember incorrectly, or Tracy could have lied."

"Why?" Nadine demanded.

It was my turn to shrug. "Well, she didn't fill out the next of kin part of her application, right? Maybe she was hiding something."

"Or maybe she was just an idiot who forgot to fill out all the information," Lorrette said. "Believe me, being a former teacher I know this for a fact — there are a lot of idiots out there."

I patted her hand. "Look, I'll talk with the captain, okay? See what I can find out. Or maybe we should do our own checking on Tracy Bishop."

"How?" Nadine demanded. "I mean, from here?"

I sighed. "I don't know," I said. "But I'll find out."

Willis and I caught up with the others at Cinnamon Bay. On the way there, I told him what

I'd found out from Lorrette and Nadine.

"That's stupid," was his first comment. "Why would the captain think that has anything to do with anything? It's a gay thing," he said. "He immediately suspects her because she's gay."

"Spoken like a true conspiracy buff, darling," I said, patting his knee. "But you could be right. On the other hand, maybe he doesn't like coincidences."

He gave me a look. "You don't like coincidences," he said.

"True," I agreed, "but they do happen."

"And in this case, you think that's all it is? A coincidence that Tracy and Lorrette lived in the same town?"

"If Tracy even came from Galveston. And even if she did, if we conducted a survey of all the hotels and motels and rental spots on this island right now, how many people do you think we'd find from Galveston?"

Willis shrugged.

"I don't know either," I said. "But it's a thought."

We pulled into the car park for the beach, which was situated in a tangle of green — heavy vines, ripe trees, wild ferns. We parked the Suzuki, grabbed our equipment, and headed for the beach, taking a path through thick greenery. As we walked through, Willis grabbed my arm and whispered, "Look!"

I followed his pointing finger. There, in a small clearing among the vines and trees, were a cat, a plain old domestic pussycat, and a mongoose — both scouring the grounds for goodies, totally ignoring each other.

"Where's the camera?" I demanded in a whisper.

Willis rummaged through his stuff until he found it. By the time he got the camera to his eye, however, the two had spied us and decided hunting might be better further into the jungle.

We continued down the path until it opened up on the beach — beautiful white sand, unbelievable blue water, the lush green backdrop, the blue of the sky. The whole thing was almost an overload to the senses. We found our group camped out under some lush trees a few yards down the beach.

The place was full, but not crowded. I lost Willis's attention for a moment as two very well tanned and big breasted young women walked by in string bikinis. I kicked him and he came back to consciousness. Then there was a young man walking by in a Speedo — a young man who I'm sure was the very model for wearing a Speedo — and Willis had to remind me who I was.

We got to our group and Liz grabbed my arm. "Did you see that?" she asked, indicating the departing Speedo.

"I may have noticed," I said grinning.

"Yowsa," my big sister said.

"You girls cool it or we're going to start noticing those string bikinis," Willis said.

130

"*Start* noticing?" Liz and I asked in unison.

Arlan wasn't with the rest of the group. Liz pointed him out standing knee-deep in the Caribbean, spitting into his goggles. Cheryl I saw lying a few feet away on a beach towel, attempting a suntan. None of the other three of us would ever do such a stupid thing, but somehow I was afraid Cheryl would be able to carry it off. Like everything else.

"Have you been out?" I asked Liz.

"Yes, and it's great." She pointed out into the water, at a small island a couple of hundred yards from the beach. "Can you see those signs in the water there? That's a snorkel path. We haven't gone out there yet, but it's supposed to be great. Some really good snorkeling they tell me."

"Y'all want to head out?" Larry asked, fins in one hand, snorkel and mask in the other.

I looked at Willis. "Let me play around in the shallow water for a little while," I said. "Then I'll head over."

"Well, stay in a buddy system," Larry said. "That's the way to do it."

We nodded and he and Liz, hand in hand, headed into the water.

"I'd like to try that path," Willis said.

"Give me a few minutes."

We got our gear and headed into the water, staying in shallows while I got my nerve up to head deeper into the bay. Finally we started out, swimming leisurely toward the beginning of the path. The path circled the small island and the signs sticking out of the water explained the coral, plants, and sea life surrounding the island.

We were at our third sign, heading toward the back of the island, when I heard a commotion. I looked up. Two men were on the little island and their voices were getting loud.

I couldn't distinguish the words, but the tone was definitely one of anger. Treading water, I took off my mask and wiped my eyes. It was a white man and a black man. The white man was holding on to the black man's arm and shaking him. The white man was wearing Bermuda shorts, socks, sandals, and no shirt, and he had a pot belly sticking out over the top of the shorts.

Even from this distance I recognized Bud George. And the younger man, the black man whose arm Bud was gripping, was none other than the guy in the dredlocks and orange flowered shorts whom I'd found staring at our house on two different occasions.

I grabbed Willis's foot, as he had moved on without me, and hauled him back to where I was treading water.

"Look," I said quietly, pulling at his mask and snorkel.

He took them off and stared where I indicated. "That's the guy!" he said.

"Yeah, and look who he's talking to," I said.

"Who is that?" Willis asked, frowning into the sun.

"Bud George," I said.

He squinted. "Naw, it can't be."

"Why not?"

"Well, why would it be?"

"Let's go in closer," I suggested, leaving the path and heading toward the island.

"E.J. —"

"Shhh," I said, doing my Esther Williams bit.

When we got close enough to the island to stand up in the water, I said to Willis, "What'd I tell you?"

"Damn, it is him! What's going on?"

The young black man had pulled his arm out of Bud's grip and was walking away. Bud grabbed him and swung him around. The young man raised a fist and neatly knocked Bud on his ass. Willis, ever my hero, yelled, "Hey, now!" and starting charging out of the water.

The young man took one look at Willis and headed around the island. By the time we got there, the youth was in the water, swimming resolutely toward shore.

Bud was struggling to get up from the sand. We went over and helped him.

"What was that all about?" Willis asked.

"That stupid nig—" He looked at me and changed his mind. "That kid was trying to rob me!" he said.

"Looked to me like *you* were holding on to *him*," Willis said.

Bud puffed up, pulling in his gut and sticking

out his sickly chest. "I don't put up with that kinda crap! Not anywhere! Not from anybody! I was giving him a piece of my mind!"

"Good way to get a piece of your mind smeared all over the beach, Bud," Willis said. "You okay?"

Bud rubbed his chin where the young black man had hit him. "Well, I'll live, I guess." He grinned. "Ain't as young as I used to be. Used to, I woulda wiped the floor with him!"

"What are you doing out here on this island anyway, Bud?" I asked.

He grinned. "Came to meet up with Arlan," he said, pointing at my hairy toad of a brother-in-law as he and his brief Speedo climbed out of the water. "Thought he could come out to the boat with me. Y'all wanna come?"

Willis and I backed off, giving our apologies, and headed back to the water.

It was then that I thought it might be a good idea to tell Willis about seeing dear old Bud with the late Tracy Bishop. I was thinking this guy got around a little too much.

SEVEN

I waited until Willis and I were alone, sitting in an open-air cafe having our first rum of the day on our way back from the beach. My skin felt sticky and tight — too much sand and too much sun. I wore a straw hat with a wide brim over my salt-water-ravaged hair, hoping to shield my face from any more sun. This close to the equator, even in early March, the sun was treacherous — even for non-redheads.

Willis took one bite of a conch fritter and tossed it back in the basket. "I swear to God if I eat one more piece of conch, I'm going to throw up," he said.

"Would you rather order calamari?" I asked.

He gave me a look.

"Sorry," I said, "I don't see chicken-fried steak on the menu."

"Mexican food," he said wistfully. "Real live TexMex. That's what I want. Cheese enchiladas and pork tamales and a big old bowl of guacamole. Your guacamole. All that stuff that's bad for my cholesterol level."

"I have to tell you something," I said.

"Does it have anything to do with something hot and greasy and readily available?"

I poked at the fritters. "These are relatively hot and greasy," I said. "But, no, it doesn't. The day before we found Tracy Bishop, the day we rented the car?"

Willis nodded.

"Remember we saw Bud George getting out of his dinghy at the dock?"

Again Willis nodded.

"Remember Arlan decided not to go talk to him because Bud was talking with someone else?"

"Yeah, so?" Willis asked, his temper getting short. And here we were, on vacation.

"I'm almost positive the woman he was talking to was Tracy Bishop."

He looked at me. "You think maybe this is all just hindsight? Admit you don't like Bud George."

"Yes, I admit I don't like Bud George, but that hasn't got anything to do with it. I thought it was the same girl at the time. Now we've got this strange young man staring at the house. We caught him twice, God only knows how many times we didn't catch him! And now Bud George having a fight with this same guy! Something is going on, Willis."

He nodded his head. "Okay, Bud killed Tracy and her boyfriend is after him."

"How did Bud get in the house?" I demanded.

"We didn't have the alarm on, remember?"

"Okay, why?"

Willis shrugged. "I did the hard part — I came up with a major suspect. You can at least work out the motive."

I went back to my rum. "You're not very good at this," I said.

"I have my moments," he countered.

I convinced Willis it would be a good idea to head into Cruz Bay before going back to the house. I needed to tell the captain about Bud George and Tracy Bishop.

"But you're not absolutely sure it *was* Tracy Bishop," Willis said, driving down the wrong side of the road — correctly.

"Yes, I am," I countered.

Willis shook his head. "Hindsight," he said.

"Hindsight this," I said and made a rude gesture.

He shook his head. "And you were such a sweet thing when I married you."

We found a parking place near police headquarters and headed up the stairs to the front door. It opened before we got there. Captain Micha Robinson was standing there, one step up, looming over both Willis and me.

"Mr. and Mrs. Pugh," he said, nodding his head. The bigger-than-life smile seemed to be missing.

"Hi, Captain," I said. "I forgot to tell you one other thing this morning —"

He looked at a slip of paper in his hand. "Oh? Like the fact that you single-handedly put a man in the hospital with multiple broken bones and contusions —"

"What?" I demanded.

"Or the fact that a body was found in your car in your driveway? And that you were a prime suspect in the murder of a teenage boy?"

"I didn't do it! That was proven —"

"Or that you and an accomplice were jailed for obstructing justice and harboring a fugitive?"

"That wasn't an accomplice, that was my mother-in—"

"How about the fact that you were the only one in your entire community to side with a child molester?" He glared at me.

"You're missing the point —"

"Well, honey, you did," Willis started.

I shot him a look.

"Where did you get all this stuff?" I demanded of the captain.

He looked at the papers in his hand. "Police Chief Catfish Watkins of Codderville, Texas, was kind enough to fax me your record."

"I don't have a record!"

He waved the fax sheet at me. "I beg to differ," he said.

"I can explain all that —"

"I'm sure you can, Mrs. Pugh. Just as I'm sure every person I've ever arrested and sent to prison was as innocent as the driven snow."

"Captain —" I started.

But he turned and walked back in the building. "Excuse me, please. I have work to do."

He slammed the door of the police station, leaving Willis and me standing on the porch.

I looked at Willis.

"Well," he said. "It's not like most of that isn't true."

"But I can explain!" I whined.

Willis put his arm around me and led me down the stairs. "I know you can, honey," he said, but his voice was dripping with condescension. I hate it when he does that.

We got back to the house to find that Nadine and Lorrette had been productive while we were all out getting burned and water-logged. Steaks and corn on the cob were on the grill, and a large tossed salad was cooling in the refrigerator. Everyone was being very cheerful and pointedly not asking Lorrette what the captain had wanted that morning.

When I got the chance I needed to tell her she wasn't the captain's only star suspect any longer. That *femme fatale* from Black Cat Ridge was definitely in the running for suspect of the month.

Willis and I took a communal shower in the open-air shower stall and changed into clean, nonsandy clothes, then went downstairs to join the others.

The doors to the deck were open and we heard the honk of a horn. Looking out, we saw

Bud and Marge George pulling their dinghy up on the rock beach in front of the house.

"They do seem to know when food is being served, don't they?" Liz whispered in my ear.

Arlan headed out to the beach to help them haul up the dinghy, and the rest of us moved leisurely out on to the deck, drinks in hand, to watch.

The sun was just beginning to set over the horizon at the mouth of the bay, and the reflection of the sky was turning the sea pink and gold. Shadows hung from the trees and danced in the slight breeze while night birds sang.

Willis was nuzzling my neck, and I was trying to come up with a good excuse to leave the party when it happened.

The flash came first. A small light against the darkening sky. Then a big ball of fire swept through the Georges' cabin cruiser out in the bay at the same time as the massive boom of sound hit us. Out on the rock beach, Marge was thrown to the ground. Other boats near the cruiser were pushed away, some hitting others moored close to them.

I'm not sure how long we all stood there transfixed. It seemed like a long time, but it couldn't have been more than seconds before I ran down to the beach where Marge lay sprawled across the rocks. Nadine was close behind me.

Arlan was holding his head and Bud was staring out at the bay. "Our stuff!" he yelled. "All our stuff!"

He appeared to be paying no attention to his wife, who was lying prostrate on the ground. When Nadine and I got to her, she was groggy but conscious, and bleeding from several cuts that seemed to come more from the rocks she had fallen on than any debris from the explosion.

Willis came down to help us. "I called the captain," he said, helping Marge sit up.

"Marge, baby, you okay?" Bud finally asked, charging in and almost knocking me down.

"Back off!" I said, giving him an elbow. "Give her some room to breathe!"

"Huh?" Bud shouted at me.

"Oh, my, oh, my," Marge was saying. "What in the world happened?"

"Our boat blew up!" Bud shouted. "You leave the gas on in the galley again?"

Marge gave her husband a withering look. "I most certainly did not, Bud George! And you just behave yourself! Can't you see I'm bleeding!" Marge began to cry — great heaving sobs. "Just look at me!" she said between sobs. "I'm bloody all over!"

Nadine helped her to her feet. "Come on in the house and let's get you cleaned up," she said. "Let me check out these cuts. I'm an RN."

Marge grabbed hold of her. "Oh, I'm just the luckiest woman in the world! A nurse right here when I need one! Only thing better would be if you were a doctor!"

Nadine laughed bitterly. "Only if you need a prescription. No doctor would wash out these wounds, I guaran-damn-tee you that!"

I helped her get Marge into the house. We could hear the sirens as we reached the deck. Some were coming from the coast guard cruiser heading into the mouth of Great Cruz Bay and some were coming from the road above, presumably as Captain Robinson headed to the house.

Liz had towels covering the sofa, so we laid Marge down there while Nadine gave orders. "Boil a pot of water, bring me scissors, a clean sheet, and, Lorrette, get that first-aid kit out of our room." The doorbell rang. "Eloise, get that," she said, obviously unable to stop giving orders even when it wasn't her domain.

I ran up the stairs and opened the door to Micha Robinson. He wasn't smiling.

"Anyone hurt?" he asked, moving past me onto the landing.

"Marge has some cuts and bruises. Nadine's treating her now. I'm not sure about Arlan. He was out on the beach when it happened and he was holding his head when we got there. I'm not sure about the other boaters out on the bay —"

"When are you people leaving my island?" he shot at me as he passed and headed down the stairs. "I've had less trouble from a houseful of fraternity boys!"

When we got downstairs Nadine was cutting

off Marge's clothes, while Marge wailed. "Those pants are brand new! I bought 'em at Neiman's! The insurance isn't gonna cover that!"

Larry and Willis were coming in the doors, both holding Arlan, whose hands were still protectively around his head.

Cheryl, who'd been standing around wringing her hands and looking pretty (her best trick), finally came to life on seeing her husband. "Arlan!" She ran to him. "Are you all right?"

He shook his head and winced.

"I don't think he can hear you," Larry said.

"That blast was damned loud!" Bud screamed from the doorway. "I think it mighta messed up ol' Arlan's ears a little bit!"

Marge lifted her head from the sofa and looked at her husband. "Bud, you're yelling!" she yelled. "Maybe something's wrong with your ears, too!"

"Huh?" Bud said.

Marge laid her head back down on the sofa. "Oh, great," she said, tears flowing freely down her face. "Now he's got a real reason for totally ignoring me!"

"Would someone tell me what happened?" Captain Robinson demanded.

Willis turned to Bud and yelled, "He wants to know what happened!"

"The boat blew up!" Bud yelled. He made a motion with his arms and said, "Boom!"

"How?" Captain Robinson shouted.

"Huh?" Bud asked.

"HOW . . . DID . . . IT . . . BLOW . . . UP?" the captain screamed.

"Well, I sure as hell don't know!" Bud shouted. "We didn't leave nothing on, did we, hon?"

Marge raised herself weakly from the couch. "Absolutely not," she said, then burst into tears. "All my shoes!" she cried. "Gone with the wind!"

Larry was still out on the deck, watching the coast guard cruiser as its fire brigade tried putting out the flames of what was left of the Georges' cabin cruiser. Other coast guard personnel were checking out the crews of the other boats moored near the burning cruiser.

"Everybody okay out there?" Captain Robinson called to Larry.

"Looks like it!" Larry called back.

"That your dinghy tied up on the beach?" he asked Bud.

Bud said, "Huh?"

The captain repeated the question at a louder decibel level and Bud nodded his head. "I want to borrow it!" the captain shouted.

Bud looked as if he were going to say something, then shrugged and handed the captain the key to the outboard.

"Nothing much left to lose, I guess," Bud shouted.

Captain Robinson took the keys and, without

a word to any of us, left the house and headed for the rocky beach.

"I don't think he's very happy with us," I said to Willis.

"Huh?" Bud shouted.

"Oh, shut up," I said under my breath.

Marge lifted her head. "I heard that, honey," she said. "Can't say I blame you." She lay back down and burst into a fresh set of tears.

Nadine was checking out Arlan's head, looking in his ears, and holding up fingers to see how many he could see. He kept batting at her hand as if not willing to play her game.

"We need to get him into Cruz Bay," Nadine said to Cheryl. "There's a doctor there. I think he needs to be looked at."

Cheryl's smooth exterior seemed to be on the verge of cracking. "I've never driven on the island," she said. She looked to Willis. "Would you drive us?"

Willis grabbed his keys and called to Larry, who was still out on the deck watching as Captain Robinson maneuvered the dinghy up to the coast guard cruiser.

"Larry, help me get Arlan up to the cars!"

"Sure thing!" Larry said, running in.

Arlan still hadn't said anything. That in itself was enough to worry me. The sight of Arlan Hawker unable to be his usual obnoxious self was a little scary. The three men headed upstairs with Cheryl following behind.

"The steaks!" Lorrette shouted and headed

out to the deck and the gas grill.

Liz, Nadine, Lorrette, and I stared at the charred remains of dinner. "Anybody like their steaks *really* well done?" Liz asked.

"Looks like take-out deli time again," I suggested.

"Who's going to drive?" Nadine asked.

We all looked at each other.

"Anybody on the island deliver?" Lorrette suggested.

"We can do it," Liz said. She looked at me. "Eloise?"

"What?" I demanded.

"You can drive."

I grinned. "Willis took our Suzuki," I said and shrugged. "Sorry."

"Larry's got the keys to ours," she said.

Then we all turned and looked at the floor next to the couch where Marge lay, dozing fitfully. Cheryl's purse was lying there.

"I'm sure Arlan has the keys to the Land Rover in his pocket," I said.

"But what if he doesn't?" Nadine said. "John used to keep all sorts of his junk in my purse when we were married." We continued to stare at the purse. "Maybe we should check."

"You check," Liz said.

"I'm not going to check," Lorrette said. "She's not *my* sister."

I sighed. "Well, I certainly have nothing to lose in the relationship department," I said. I walked over to the couch and picked Cheryl's purse up from the floor, trying to be quiet enough not to awaken Marge. Anything was better than Marge George awake.

Cheryl's purse was a very casual woven straw Louis Vuitton beach bag. My neighbor Luna and I had seen one just like it at a pricey store in Austin on a shopping trip one Saturday. I remember distinctly laughing with Luna over who in the world would pay $610 for a beach bag. I'd have to remember to tell her just *who* would.

I shook the bag and heard something rattle.

"Those have to be keys," Liz whispered, coming up beside me — obviously as anxious as I was to keep Marge asleep.

"They're probably her house keys," I whispered back.

"Well, check, for God's sake," Nadine said a little too loudly.

I thrust the purse at her. "You check."

Lorrette finally grabbed the bag from me. "You people!" she said and thrust her hand into the purse. She pulled out a set of keys with the Land Rover emblem on them. *"Voila!"* she whispered loudly, holding the keys aloft.

"Now who's going to drive?" Nadine asked as the four of us moved away from the couch and the now snoring Marge George.

"Eloise is," Liz and Lorrette said in unison.

"Why me?" I whined.

"Because you're the youngest," Liz said, turning me around by the shoulders and pushing me toward the stairs. "So you'll have better reflexes."

When Willis and I lived in Mexico, we were held at gunpoint by banditos until they realized we had no money but were willing to share our dope. A few years ago, after my daughter Bessie's birth parents were killed, the killers snuck into our house and tried to kill me and my children. Not too long ago I opened the back door of my car to let my children inside and discovered a naked dead body. I once jumped in a winter cold river to save a suicidal teenager, and even drove into the motorcycle gang/speed lab section of town in the wee hours of the night to interview a drug-crazed murder suspect named Tiny. And I won't even mention the bloody pumpkin head.

But none of that — none of it — was as scary as driving that huge Land Rover down the wrong side of those crazy, narrow streets of St. John. Especially with three women yelling in my ears, "Watch out!" every other turn. And believe me, there were a lot of turns from that fabulous house to the town of Cruz Bay.

But I made it. To the store and back again. Yet I refused to take the Land Rover down the steep driveway and attempt to park it.

"You can't leave it up here!" Nadine shouted as I bailed from the car, keys in the ignition and motor running.

"Yes, I can!" I said, grabbing a bag of take-out and heading for the front door. "You guys are on your own!"

I went inside the house and down to the kitchen, ignoring the situation I'd left behind.

Therefore, I can state unequivocally, here and in a court of law if necessary, that I have no idea where that crease in the bumper of the Land Rover came from. I *can* state, however, that my sister Liz was the first one in the door and the first one to grab the bottle of rum off the drainboard. The fact that she drank it straight from the bottle is something I'll try to keep to myself.

I saw the dinghy heading back to the beach. Liz and I went out to meet Captain Robinson.

"Is everybody okay out there?" I asked as he pulled the dinghy up on the beach.

"No major injuries," he said. "Minor cuts and bruises. But the cabin cruiser is a goner."

"Would you like to stay for dinner?" Liz asked. "We burned the steaks, but we have plenty of deli take-out."

"No thank you," the captain said, his manner formal. "I must be getting back." He sighed and looked at us. "You people must tell me everything you know! You know that, don't you? No secrets!"

Liz and I looked at each other. "We're not keeping any secrets!" I said. "I swear!"

He gave me a look that indicated he suspected the truth of my statement. And I swear I wasn't lying! Not at all, for a change.

"Honestly, Captain," Liz said. "We've told you everything!"

Nadine and Lorrette came out on the deck. The captain looked levelly at Lorrette. "You keep your secrets," he said. "All of you. I'm just not sure which of you killed the girl — or if you all did it."

With that, he turned and walked up the outside stairs to the car park, leaving my sisters and me staring open-mouthed after him.

EIGHT

Arlan had a concussion, but no shattered eardrums as Nadine had feared. We took turns staying up with him in the upstairs master bedroom. I had the 3 to 6 a.m. shift and wasn't all that happy about it.

Cheryl was sleeping on the couch in the living room while the Georges — invited by someone in our group (I'm betting Cheryl but she's not admitting it) — were camped out on the sofabed in the dining area. We all loaned them toiletries and clothes, and I could only hope they'd find a room at a nice hotel by no later than noon the next day.

Willis had the Arlan-sitting shift right before me and wasn't terribly gracious with his elbow in my ribs to wake me up.

"Your turn," he said, falling onto his pillow.

"Um," I said, rolling back over. I got the elbow again.

"Personally, I don't care if Arlan croaks or not," he said, "but you're the one who's going to have to tell Cheryl, not me."

I crawled out of bed, found my robe, and tied

it over my pajamas. The pajamas weren't much — not revealing in any way — but I'm sure my brother-in-law the Toad would come up with something lewd to say if I came in the room clad only in them, concussion or no concussion.

This was my first viewing of the upstairs master bedroom. It was even bigger and better appointed than the master bedroom we didn't get downstairs. The oversized king bed was in the middle of the room with a free-standing back of teak that had built-in electric outlets, lights, CD controls, TV controls, and a switch to open the skylight from totally closed and dark, to open to the Plexiglass dome, or to open to the air.

The wraparound windows had a view as good (okay, maybe a little better) than ours, with built-in dressers, a chest with a large-screen TV and expensive stereo equipment, and a large free-standing sunken tub in the middle of the room, with its own skylight. A large dressing area/bathroom was off that, and beyond the bathroom was a door to their outdoor shower, complete with a nosy iguana whom Cheryl said liked to watch her take a shower. One could only assume it was a male iguana.

The Toad — I mean Arlan — was sitting up in bed *sans* shirt, or at least I finally figured that out after realizing he wasn't wearing a brown mohair sweater to bed. He grinned at me when I walked in.

"Well, hell, honey, this is sure better than Willis! Come to play with me for a while?"

I smiled weakly. "Hey, Arlan," I said. "How're you feeling?"

"Huh?" he said, craning his head.

I didn't want to scream at him and wake up the rest of the house, so I found a pad of paper and wrote him a note.

"Oh, pretty good," he said, then pointed to his ears. "My hearing's coming back a little, but it's still kinda distorted."

I wrote, "Want to play a game?"

He leered at me. "Now, sweetheart, what did you have in mind?"

I took the paper, drew a hangman's scaffold, put some blanks down, carefully filling in the vowels, and handed it to him. He scowled. "Not my idea of a good time," he said.

I just stared at him. He sighed and handed me the pad back. "B," he said. Gleefully I hung a head from the scaffold.

Bud's and Arlan's hearing slowly returned the next day, and Marge was really nothing more than sore, other than, of course, suffering the mental anguish of having lost all her shoes.

Marge walked slowly around the house, stiff-armed and stiff-legged, moaning softly to herself and wanting to be waited on. "I sure would like a cool drink," she said at one point, slouched on the sofa in the living room and staring aimlessly at nothing. She sighed. "A cool drink and maybe a damp cloth for my head."

I tiptoed out of the room before she saw me.

As far as I was concerned, however, things were definitely out of hand. I needed to make a phone call, but the only phone in the house was in the kitchen, and the kitchen never seemed to be empty of people. I stole upstairs to the room Willis and I shared and got my cell phone out of my purse. I didn't want to think of the cost of a call from the Virgin Islands to Texas, but like Scarlett, I'd worry about it tomorrow.

I dialed the number of the Codderville PD and asked to speak to Elena Luna, my next-door neighbor and a detective on that force. Having to give my name before the officer who answered the phone would put me through, Luna answered with, "I hear you're in trouble yet again."

"That's not true," I said. "I had nothing to do with it."

"You're a magnet," she said. "No, no, better analogy. You're the Bermuda Triangle of homicide. Wherever you go, you suck the homicidal into your wake."

"Very poetic," I said. "Can we talk?"

"You should have seen Catfish gathering up the info to send to that island cop. He was actually giggling! Very cute, really."

"We've got a problem here, Luna," I said sternly.

"Yeah, right. Dead body in the pool. So what else is new?" she said. Her attention, as always,

154

seemed to be on something else.

"Not in the pool," I corrected. "In the cistern, which was in the living room, if you can believe it."

"Huh," she said, ignoring me.

"The point is," I said, "the captain thinks one of us did it!"

"Surprise, surprise."

"Luna! I need your help!"

"Should I mention that at best I'm thousands of miles away from you at the moment, thank God, and at the worst, I don't really care?"

"I need Catfish Watkins to send another fax to the captain explaining that I'm an upright citizen! That I've actually helped your department —"

"Ha!" she interrupted.

"Hey, now! It's true! You have to admit it's true."

"No, I don't."

"Luna, the captain won't even speak to me now. He thinks I'm some sort of loony. I think he thinks we all are."

"And your point is?"

I sighed and gritted my teeth. "I know you're having all sorts of fun with this, Luna, but I really need Catfish to retract or at least explain what he told the captain!"

Luna sighed in return. "Okay, okay. I doubt if I can get him to do it," she said. "He was having such a good time. But I'll see what I can do."

"Promise me?"

"Hey, I'm not promising you squat!" she said. "I'll talk to him. That's all."

"Ah, one more thing, Luna," I said.

There was a silence that lasted so long I don't even want to think how much it cost me cellular-wise. Finally she said, "What?"

"There's a cop in Houston who's supposed to be checking out this girl's apartment." I wracked my brain trying to come up with the cop's name. "Price or Pierce. No! Pearson! David Pearson! Houston homicide. The victim's name was Tracy Bishop. Would you call —"

"No," she said with no hesitation whatsoever.

"Luna, I'm on my cell phone. You know eventually you'll do this for me after I badger you for forty-five minutes. Unfortunately, after the cost of this trip, I won't be able to afford the cell phone bill when it comes in! So let's just cut to the chase and say you'll do it for me."

"God, you're a pain in the ass."

"I know, I know. Yada, yada, yada. Now you'll do it?"

"I doubt if he'll —"

"Of course he will! You're a fellow cop. Just do it and let me get off the phone, okay?"

"On one condition," she said.

"Name it."

"You wash my toilets once a week for a month. All three of them."

"Luna!"

"Deal?"

Lord, was this girl having fun or what? I sighed. "Whatever," I said.

"Deal?" she insisted.

"Yes, yes! It's a deal! You'll do it?"

"Give me your cell phone number again. I left it at home. I'll call you back. That's gonna cost you too, right? I don't have to pay at this end? Or do I call you collect or what?"

The honest answer was I had no idea. I'm not sure that was covered in my cell phone handbook, and even if it was, that was at home and I was here. "No, just dial direct and it'll be charged to my cell phone," I said, sounding, I hoped, convincing. "Or you can bring me the information," I suggested. "You feel like coming out to the island?"

"Ha! You finally admit you need me!"

"Not at all. Just thought you could use some sun," I said, thanked her profusely, and hung up, hoping there would be a big fat charge on the Codderville PD phone bill at the end of the month that Luna was going to have some fun explaining.

I wandered to the windows, looking out at the bay. The scar that had been the Georges' boat had been removed. The others moored out there looked peaceful enough, as if nothing had happened the day before.

A slight noise to the right made me turn and look out the windows overlooking the car park.

He was there again. The beautiful guy in the dredlocks and orange shorts, although this day he was wearing cutoff jeans and a T-shirt. And he was doing something he shouldn't be doing to the Land Rover.

I ran through the bathroom and out the door to the stairs leading to the car park, yelling the entire way. Before I got to the top of the steps, the dredlocked young man was bounding up the hill to the road, crushing bougainvillea and wild orchids as he went. Doors opened all over the house and my family streamed out.

Willis caught up with me first. "What happened?" he demanded.

"It was him again!" I said, pointing at the fleeing figure almost out of sight now. "He was messing with the Land Rover."

Arlan had joined us. "What was he doing?"

I shrugged. "I'm not sure."

We all approached the big car with uncertainty. Finally, Willis got on his back and scooted under the car, looking, I suppose, for a bomb. He didn't find one. Gingerly, he opened the hood. Arlan and Larry joined him, as if being male gave them inside knowledge on the workings of the combustion engine. And for all I knew it did.

Nadine, the nurse, the trained observer, was the one who found it. "Look," she said, pointing on the ground near the back of the Land Rover. We all stood around staring at where she was pointing. At first I didn't see anything. Then Nadine squatted down on the ground and stuck her finger on small white granules that were noticeable against the cobblestones. Gingerly, she touched her tongue to her finger, then looked up at Willis. "Sugar," she said.

The point of spillage was squarely beneath the gas tank. Arlan opened the flap of the gas tank. More granules were to be found there, and the screw-on top of the tank wasn't totally closed. I'd caught him before he was able to put it back correctly, maybe even caused him to spill a little of the sugar.

"Who in the hell *is* this guy?" Arlan demanded.

"And why in the hell is he doing this?" Willis added. He turned to look at Bud, who was standing behind him. "So, Bud? Who is he?"

Bud's eyes got huge. "How the hell should I know?"

"He was the one you were fighting with on the island," I said.

"I tole you! The guy was trying to rob me! Looks like he's a real nut!"

"I think it's about time you explained to us what you were doing talking with Tracy Bishop the day before she died," I said.

All eyes turned to me, then quickly to Bud. "Huh?" he said.

I just stared at him.

He shook his head. "I don't know what you're talking about. Who's Tracy whatever? That colored girl who died? Why would I be talking to her?"

"Exactly my point," I said.

Bud shook his head. "Don't know what you're talking about, Eloise. I think it's damn rude of you to suggest such a thing," he said, sucking in his belly and sticking out his chest. "I'm a happily married man and I don't go around diddlin' with colored girls. Or any other girls," he said, directing this last remark to Marge.

"He most certainly does not," Marge said, coming to her husband's defense. She moved next to him and stuck her arm through his. "I think we've worn out our welcome here, Bud. I think we should go find us a nice hotel."

"I think you're right, honey," he said, and the two of them marched off for the house.

Cheryl looked at me and shook her head. "My God, Eloise, you are a piece of work, aren't you? Don't you ever stop playing Nancy Drew?"

She turned and followed the Georges into the house. Liz and Nadine looked at me. "Did you really see him talking to Tracy Bishop?" Liz asked.

"You're right!" Larry said. "I remember! He was talking to someone on the beach. Remember?" he said, turning to Willis. "Arlan was going up to him and then stopped and said, 'He's busy,' or something like that. He was with a woman. A black woman."

"Was it Tracy?" Liz demanded.

Larry shrugged. "Ah, that I don't know."

"Believe me," I said, "it was Tracy."

Nadine giggled and rubbed her hand [to]gether. "Oh, this just keeps getting bette[r and] better," she said.

Well, my Nancy Drew-ing did have one [posi]tive result — the Georges moved out of [the] house. Cheryl wasn't speaking to me, but [she] didn't seem to speak to anyone really. [She] spent most of her time sitting on the sofa in [the] living room, reading beauty magazines or do[ing] her nails. Intellectually, I didn't think Che[ryl] had changed much since junior high.

It was Thursday. We were supposed to lea[ve] the island on Sunday. I was worried that, ev[en] as much as Captain Robinson would like to s[ee] us gone, he wouldn't let us leave the islan[d] until there was some resolution to Trac[y] Bishop's murder.

The key to the whole thing had to be th[e] dredlocked young black man. Either he was the killer who kept returning for some strange reason to the scene of the crime, or he knew who the killer was. And the fact that he had ac-costed Bud George on the small island in Cin-namon Bay made me wonder once again about Bud George. Maybe it was a good thing he and Marge had left the house for a hotel for more reasons than just the annoyance factor. Maybe we were all a little safer having him further away.

I *knew* it was Tracy Bishop that Bud had

been talking to that day. Willis might have his doubts about my memory, and so might the captain about my motives — but *I knew* it had been the murdered girl I'd seen with Bud George just a day before her death. So Bud George was in this up to his bushy eyebrows. But into what I didn't know. Did he kill her? If so, why? What was his connection to my brother-in-law Larry's dental receptionist?

I was pondering all this on the deck while I watched the sun slowly sink into the Caribbean. I was drinking Diet Coke for a change, hoping to flush out some of the rum I'd been soaking my body in for the past few days. Paradise or not, it was time for me to get serious about this whole thing. A young woman was dead, a boat had been blown up, and the captain of police for the island of St. John suspected one or all of us. I didn't need booze clogging my brain, or even the great sunset obscuring my thinking. If we were ever going to leave this island (and in my heart I knew I had to eventually), someone was going to have to find out who killed Tracy Bishop.

I felt lips on my neck. I turned and gave my husband a kiss.

"What say we blow this pop stand?" Willis said.

"What do you have in mind?" I asked.

"One of the coast guard guys yesterday was telling me about this great restaurant in Cruz Bay. A French chef, the whole bit. I thought I'd

take my lady out for an evening."

"Give me twenty minutes to change," I said, and ran into the house and up the stairs.

I wore a pale yellow, spaghetti-strapped sundress, a pair of semi-decent sandals, and my pearls. My husband, decked out in a floral patterned shirt he'd bought on our shopping spree in Cruz Bay, declared me beautiful. I accepted the compliment as my due.

We told the others, who were busy discussing what should be done with the Land Rover and its sugar-filled tank, we were leaving, without giving any specifics (we didn't want company), and headed for our Suzuki.

As we drove the narrow, winding streets of Cruz Bay, reggae music was blaring loudly from the different bars we passed as we headed for the restaurant. The restaurant was interesting — by day it was a fast-food hamburger joint, by night a three-star French bistro. It was on the second floor of the building, all of it open air. We hadn't been in a restaurant or bar yet in Cruz Bay that hadn't been open air.

I slipped into the restroom shortly after we were seated. I only mention this because a sign in the restroom, to me, summed up the island of St. John to a tee. It read, IN THIS LAND OF FUN AND SUN, WE DON'T FLUSH FOR NUMBER ONE.

Leaving the toilet unflushed, as instructed, I

headed for the table, feeling a little guilty and slightly amused.

The menu boasted such entrees as duck in orange sauce, mahi-mahi in lemon butter, shrimp stuffed with crab and crab stuffed with shrimp, and a host of things I didn't readily recognize. We ordered stuffed mushrooms and escargot for appetizers, duck with rice and an endive salad for me, mahi-mahi with new potatoes and seafood gumbo for Willis. I was still eating my appetizers and perusing the dessert menu when the people at the table next to us got up to leave. They were barely away from the table when the busboy came to clear.

I almost choked on an escargot. Willis heard my intake of breath and looked up. Before the dredlocked young black man could move, Willis had him by the arm and was pulling him to a chair at our table.

It was my first really close look at him. He appeared to be about nineteen or twenty, baby-faced, and beautiful, except for the scowl that played across his face. He was as tall as Willis, although more slimly built.

Willis's scowl matched that of the younger man. "Just shut up and sit down if you don't want to lose your job," my husband hissed. " 'Cause believe me, I'll make a scene so loud nobody on this island will hire you," Willis said. The young man sat, glaring at both of us.

"What's going on?" I asked him.

He didn't answer.

"You've got one minute and I start yelling pickpocket. You got that?" Willis said.

"I don't know what you're talking about," he said.

There was no accent. This guy was an American, not an islander.

"Who are you?" I asked.

He glared at me. "My name's Jacob," he said.

"How are you connected to Tracy Bishop?" I asked.

"Who?" he said.

Willis squeezed his arm. "Don't give me that shit!" he said, his teeth gritted. "Answer the question."

Jacob pulled his arm away from Willis and stood up, knocking his chair backward. "You wanna cost me this job, man, that's fine. I don't have to talk to you or your woman! Or any of you people! You're all killers! Every damn one of you and I hope you all rot in hell!"

He walked out of the restaurant, presumably giving up the job of his own accord. Those patrons not watching Jacob's exit were watching us. Willis stood up to follow him, but I pressed his arm, asking him to sit back down. "What more do you think you're going to get out of him?" I asked. "He thinks we're the enemy."

"You think he was Tracy's boyfriend?" Willis asked, sitting down and ignoring the stares of our fellow diners.

I shrugged. "Something. He was obviously connected to her and he thinks we killed her."

"Because her body was found in our house," Willis said.

I shrugged again. "Well, can you blame him?"

"We need to tell the captain about him," Willis said.

I sighed. "He's not exactly welcoming any news from us," I said.

Willis flagged down our waiter. When the young American college student came to our table, Willis asked, "That young man who just left — with the dredlocks. Jacob?"

Our waiter nodded. "What's his last name?" Willis asked.

"Bishop," the waiter said. "Jacob Bishop."

It was dark before we started back to the house. Neither of us really wanted to go. When Willis suggested a detour to one of the island beaches, I readily agreed.

We parked the Suzuki and got out, taking off our shoes and wading in the gentle, warm Caribbean.

"Her husband?" Willis asked.

"I guess," I said. "Or some kind of relative."

The sky was black velvet sprinkled liberally with sequins. We didn't really live in a city back home — just a very large subdivision — but we still didn't have stars like this in Black Cat Ridge. Everything here seemed closer, bigger, more real than it did at home — while at the same time seeming surrealistically unreal.

Lights from the beach bar of the Westin Hotel bounced off the water and laughter echoed across the bay. Willis put his arms around me and pulled me to him. "Next time, we do this with just the two of us," he said. "And if you even mention a member of your family, I'll throw you in the bay."

"What family?" I asked, nuzzling his neck.

"And no murders. We don't speak to another soul. So if anyone does get killed, we won't even care. No skin off our noses."

"Murder? What murder?" I breathed in his ear.

"Nobody here but us chickens," he said, and kissed me.

Willis and I have been married a long time, and when you have children and a house and animals and a mortgage and in-laws and neighbors, you tend to get in a bit of a rut when it comes to love-making. The meet-you-at-ten-o'clock-your-side-of-the-bed scenario. But St. John was liberating. There were no kids, no animals, and the mortgage be damned. We made love on the beach under a palm tree, just as we'd done fifteen years before in Mexico. Okay, maybe I was a little fatter and Willis a little stiffer, but, all in all, I can report it went quite well.

"She's special," Mother said.

"All my girls are special," Daddy said.

"Henry, don't be dense! I mean special," Mother said.

167

I was sitting on the landing at the head of the stairs, peeking down at my parents in the living room as they had their nightly discussion. I couldn't have been more than five or six, because I was wearing the Winnie-the-Pooh pajamas I outgrew in the first grade.

Daddy shook the newspaper and raised his reading glasses to the bridge of his nose. "Those doctors don't know anything," he said, dismissing Mother.

"We have to do something!" Mother said.

"My girls are all special!" Daddy said. He turned and glared at Mother. "And I don't want to hear another word about this! Do you hear me?"

I woke up drenched in sweat. It hadn't been a dream, but a memory. They were crowding in now, more of them every night. I definitely remembered the Winnie-the-Pooh pajamas. But I had thought at the time that Mother was talking about me. I was special. I was her youngest. It had made sense then.

But now I could see those words in another context. Special. In Mother's euphemistic world that had another meaning entirely: One of her girls had been diagnosed by a doctor as "special." Mentally retarded? Slow? Learning disabled?

It didn't make any sense. I couldn't remember any of us having to go to special classes, therapy of any kind — speech or otherwise. Was it just a dream? Or was it a memory?

I got out of bed and stared out the windows at the bay and boats below. I loved this room, this view, this house, but it was coming with a higher price tag than $1,000 a day. Murder not withstanding, I was having to deal with a lot more family shit than I'd ever wanted to.

College, then Willis, had been my ticket out. Away from an overprotective mother with negligible yet terribly in-your-face parenting skills; away from a father who had always been barely there anyway; away from my sisters Liz and Nadine who treated me like a long forgotten stepchild; and especially away from Cheryl. Cheryl the self-centered; Cheryl the beautiful; Cheryl the pain in the ass.

And Cheryl the special? I couldn't remember Cheryl ever reading a book. Only magazines with slick pictures. She hadn't done that well in school, but her looks got her by when her smarts would not have. She was the only one of us who didn't go to college. So? That meant nothing. Lots of smart people didn't go to college.

But Cheryl wasn't smart. She was savvy and manipulative, but she wasn't smart.

I left our room and went downstairs, knocking gently on the door to Liz and Larry's room.

Liz opened the door, pulling her blue silk kimono around her. "Jesus, Eloise! It's after three!"

"We have to talk," I said, nodding my head toward the kitchen. She followed me. I started

169

a pot of coffee and fixed us two cups, then sat down with her on the sofa in the dining area.

Liz yawned. "What's up?"

"I have to ask you something — something about the family."

Liz raised an eyebrow. "Our family?" She laughed. "I thought we were an open book."

"I have a vague memory of mother telling Daddy that one of us had been diagnosed when we were little as, well, as Mother put it, 'special.' "

Liz looked away from me.

I put a hand on her bony knee. "Lizzie, it was Cheryl, right?"

She shrugged. "It was a long time ago, Eloise —"

"Liz!"

She sighed. "I don't know. There was this one time, I was about fourteen or fifteen, I guess Cheryl would have been, what? Eight or nine? Anyway, I stayed home from school sick with the cramps, and Mother had to take Cheryl to the doctor, but you remember how Mother was. She'd never leave us alone in the house. So I had to go with them." She pulled the robe tighter around her body and stared out the windows at the bay beyond. "Cheryl's teacher told Mother she needed to be tested." Liz turned to face me. "Looking back on it now, I think it was a form of dyslexia. She couldn't read. The doctor wanted to put her in a special class, get her special glasses, all that

170

stuff, but Daddy wouldn't have it. He kept saying there was nothing wrong with Cheryl, wouldn't even let Mother talk about it. I don't think I would have known about the outcome except Mother was so upset with Daddy she actually talked to me about it." Liz shrugged. "I told her she should just do it anyway. To heck with Daddy."

I shook my head. "Not Mother's style."

"She could badger him into just about anything," Liz said, "except that."

"Did Cheryl ever learn to read?" I asked.

Liz looked at me. "I have no idea, Eloise. You know we never talked about it after that." She smiled. "That's how the Marshalls handle everything: Don't talk about it and it will go away."

"Like the time I cut Cheryl's hair," I said.

Liz shivered. "Jesus, you talked about it!" She looked at the ceiling. "Hum," she said, "the roof hasn't caved in. Imagine that!"

"So she never got any help?" I persisted.

"Not that I know of, and of course, I've never asked her. I'm not even sure she's aware of anything wrong. I suppose if she can't read, she knows that, but not why. And not that Daddy kept her from getting treated."

"And I always thought Mother was the big bad wolf," I said.

"Neither of them are, Eloise. Haven't you figured that out yet? You've got three kids of your own — you should know. We all do what we think is the best for our kids. Hell, for all you know, twenty years from now you'll find out therapy was the worst thing you could have done for Bessie after her parents died."

"I doubt that," I said.

"Remember when my oldest Angie got into trouble with drugs? We put her in one of those places where everybody was sending their kids back in the eighties for drug abuse. While she was in there, one of the counselors seduced her. Larry and I thought we were doing the best for our daughter. Turns out we took her out of the frying pan and threw her in the fire ourselves. Luckily Angie was able to pull herself up by her own bootstraps. She didn't rely on Larry and me. She's a wonderful woman now and a good mother, no thanks to her parents."

"You didn't know —"

"Exactly my point! Either did Daddy!"

"Daddy didn't do something that backfired, Liz. He did nothing! It's not the same thing."

"Parenting is parenting, Eloise. You do what you think is the best for your kids and just pray that you're half right."

"And meanwhile Cheryl's suffered her entire life —"

Liz laughed. "Cheryl? Does she look like she's suffering? Honey," she said, patting my hand, "don't get all weepy on Cheryl's account. That girl could buy and sell all of us, and unfortunately, with her personality, I'm afraid she'd just sell us and not to a particularly nice buyer."

I laughed. "I think you called *me* catty the other day?" I said.

"Well, you were. I'm just being truthful." She kissed me on the cheek. "I'm going to bed and I suggest you do the same."

I watched her walk out of the kitchen and wondered how right she was, and how much Cheryl had really paid for our father's head-in-the-sand attitude.

NINE

"We need to do *something* together," Cheryl whined. "Mother is going to ask us if we did *anything* together!"

"We can always lie," Liz said, sitting at the breakfast table with her third cup of coffee.

"Well, I've been looking at the map," Lorrette said, "and there's a sugar mill ruin not too far away. Catherineberg. It's supposed to be a mild hike up to the mill and then these great views — and of course the sugar mill."

"Hike?" Nadine groused. "Uphill?"

"It's one of the tamer routes, honey," Lorrette assured her.

"Hike?" Nadine repeated, obviously still not totally convinced.

"I'm up for it," Willis said. "You know, I took up rock climbing a while back —" he started. But I shot him a look and he ended lamely with, "Sounds like fun."

Yes, two years ago Willis tried rock climbing. After spending entirely too much money on toys, and with the help of strangers, he made it up Enchanted Rock in the Texas Hill Country.

A nice little adventure, except it ended up almost costing both of us our lives.

He hadn't been rock climbing since, so I wasn't sure he could actually claim to have "taken up rock climbing." Somehow that seems to indicate an ongoing experience.

"I don't think there's any rock climbing at Catherineberg," Lorrette said.

"I didn't bring my gear," he said and shrugged, not mentioning I'd sold the entire mess at a garage sale — which I'm pretty sure I told him.

"I'm up for a hike," I said. I looked at Cheryl. "Does that sound like a nice family outing?"

She sighed. "Not if Nadine is going to bitch the entire time."

Nadine threw her arms in the air. "All right already! I give up! I'll go!" She looked pointedly at Cheryl. "And I promise not to bitch."

"That's all anyone's asking, Nadine," Cheryl said, rising from her stool and heading upstairs.

Liz leaned over and whispered in my ear, "You think she has a 'hiking up to a sugar mill ruin' ensemble?"

"I'm not taking any bets," I said, heading for the stairs and my own ensemble.

My attire consisted of cutoff blue jeans, a new St. John T-shirt, socks, my Reeboks, and my big floppy hat. Nadine wore long pants but was otherwise attired the same as me, Lorrette, and Liz. I was glad I hadn't taken Liz's bet when Cheryl finally emerged from the upstairs master suite to join us at the front door.

Her bottom was beautifully squeezed into aqua Spandex shorts, her breasts embraced by a matching aqua Spandex sports bra. Her hair was in a perfect ponytail on top of which she wore an aqua visor that matched the Spandex wonder. She wore top-of-the-line, brand new-looking Nikes on her feet, with those horrible little socklets with the pompoms on the back to keep them from sliding into your shoes. I hate those things. On me the pompoms go inside my shoes anyway, causing bumps, blisters, and general torture. I knew, however, that they would never dare to do that to Cheryl.

The ordinary sisters smiled weakly at the top-of-the-line sister and we all headed out to the cars, finally settling on two for the trip — Liz and Larry with us in one of the Suzukis, Nadine and Lorrette riding in the back of the Land Rover with Cheryl and Arlan. Luckily, we didn't have to worry about the Georges.

We maneuvered the winding, narrow roads, heading in the same direction we'd gone to Cinnamon Bay. Taking a turnoff before the beach, we found the sign for Catherineberg Sugar Mill Ruin. We parked in the parking lot and got out, grouping together at the start of the trail.

Nadine looked up at the long, winding, narrow trail ahead of us, wooden stairs interspersed at the steeper elevations. I'll give her credit — she looked for a long time, but she didn't say a word.

Finally we all headed out. I'm about as athletic as Nadine, so the two of us held up the rear, protecting the troops from any assault from below. In fifteen minutes our party reached the peak and the Catherineberg ruins. In an additional ten minutes, Nadine and I joined them.

Willis put his arm around my shoulders. "You're out of shape, honey," he said.

I gasped, "Shut up," and kept walking.

They were definitely ruins, but in my opinion, if you've seen one broken-down building you've just about seen them all. This one was rock, with some walls still standing, and some of the foundation. Signs explained what the mill had done in its heyday. I was more interested in the strange vegetation that grew out of the rock walls and foundations.

I'd bought a legend on our earlier shopping spree that was plastic coated for use while snorkeling. It showed pictures of and named the plant, animal, and sea life of the island. At a junction of wall and floor grew what appeared to be pinguin plant, also known as a wild pineapple, and by the front of the ruin I saw a wattapama — a wild-looking, spiky lavenderish plant. A termite nest hung in a genip tree outside the ruins.

I was proud of my newfound knowledge and

more than willing to share it, but everyone I approached seemed more interested in crumbling rock walls — even my husband.

I wandered on to the cliff at the crest of the hill on which the ruins stood. Wild sea grape cascaded down the side of the cliff, and the view of blue Caribbean was breathtaking. From my vantage point, I could see the park, a brilliant dark green next to the turquoise of the sea. The sky was darkening with storm clouds. The sun peeked out from behind a particularly dark cloud, its rays streaking through the clouds in brilliant colors. The contrasts of color and light made me long for the ability to paint. To put this on canvas could be my life's accomplishment, although I doubted anyone could duplicate the colors — the real colors of this island paradise.

I was staring off at the sights of the island, my camera at the ready, when I heard a commotion to my right. I looked over toward a stand of West Indian locusts that jutted out over the cliff and saw Arlan, and the mystery man who had been stalking our house.

The young man had his arms locked around Arlan's neck and was pushing him toward the cliff. I screamed. The two players stopped their struggle as the entire group ran toward the cliff where all the action was. The young man threw Arlan to the ground and ran off. Willis chased him, but not far. He was a little out of shape himself.

We ran to Arlan, who was struggling to right himself.

"What happened?" I demanded.

"Hell if I know!" he said, getting to his feet. "I was just checking out this view when that asshole came up behind me! I think he was trying to throw me off the cliff!"

Cheryl put her arms around her husband. "Let's get back to the car, honey," she said, shooting Lorrette a withering look. "This was a great idea!" she said.

Lorrette looked at the rest of us in horror. "How is this my fault?" she asked.

"It isn't, honey," Nadine said, putting her arm around her partner. "Consider the source."

One more point in the negative column for family bonding.

"Do you use *any* cream on your face, Eloise?" Cheryl asked me later that day at lunch, a frown on her pretty face. "I have a nightly regimen I'd tell you about," she said, "but I doubt if you could afford it. There are some things you can buy at the drug store or supermarket that would help a little."

My concern of the night before for my "special" sister was fast evaporating — she was still a bitch. Excuse me, make that Bitch with a capital "B."

I smiled a tight smile. "I'm fine, Cheryl," I said, going back to my sandwich.

"And you do know that mayonnaise is terrible for a woman your age, don't you?" she said. "So much fat is bad for the skin. Not to mention your weight."

Nadine, sitting on the other side of me on the stools at the bar, put a hand on my knee in an attempt to keep me from killing our sister.

I laughed. "I'm so busy with my career and family, Cheryl, I don't have that much time to worry about my skin." I looked at her chest. Nice, but definitely flatter than mine. "And I guess I'm lucky that my husband likes breasts."

Cheryl laughed back. "Ever heard the expression, 'Too much of a good thing'?"

"No, but can you spell it?" I spat out.

All eyes were on me. Jesus, it was just like the hair thing all over again. As far as my sister Cheryl was concerned, my buttons were large and lit with neon so she'd have no trouble pushing them.

I patted Cheryl on the arm. "Why don't you tell me what you use on your skin?" I asked. "I think it's time I started doing that."

Cheryl shrugged. "That's all I was saying," she said, then went into a learned accounting of what creams to use when. "You definitely need an exfoliant," she said, studying my pores, "and some eye cream, although it's probably too late. I have a friend who uses Preparation H for evening," she said beaming at me.

My mouth was all around a scathingly brittle yet amusing rejoinder having to do with assholes and eyeballs, but I reminded myself I was trying to be nice.

"It may be too late to do anything about your face except cover it with makeup," she said, studying me more closely than my OB/GYN ever had. "But your body skin looks pretty good." She ran her silken fingers up and down my arm. "A little dry, but nothing some good bath oils can't cure."

I smiled weakly.

There had to be a way to work this out with Cheryl — to find the sister lurking inside that pristine, cold beauty. It wasn't Cheryl's fault if she had a learning disability, and it wasn't her fault if our father was too proud and too stubborn to have it corrected when she was a child. God only knew how much of Cheryl's personality, or lack thereof, was a result of that early childhood problem.

I was an educated adult with empathy for everybody and their brother. Everybody, that is, except my own sister. Wasn't it time I tried to find her?

I grabbed a piece of paper and a pencil and began to write down the names of creams.

"You have lovely eyes, Eloise," Cheryl said. "If you wore a little color on your lids it would really enhance them. Want to come to my room and look at some of my stuff?" she asked, her demeanor more animated than it had been the entire trip.

The thought of playing makeup with Cheryl

was enough to gag me, but I had to think how much I was willing to sacrifice for this long-lost sisterhood thing. All in all, when you really thought about it, what was a few minutes of torture in the huge scheme of things?

I said, "Sure," and we left the kitchen, leaving behind the dirty dishes for the others to clean.

Liz avoided my eyes, but Nadine was clearly dumbfounded by the whole thing. I had a feeling we would be discussed as soon as we were out of earshot.

The upstairs master suite was just as luxurious as it had been the night before, but this time we went directly to the huge bathroom where there was a long counter with all Cheryl's makeup artfully spread out. There were more jars, bottles, and tubes than I'd ever seen for a single person. I felt like I was at the Clinique counter at a department store, except Cheryl wasn't wearing a white lab coat. She indicated I take the small stool in front of the mirrors while she pulled up another chair to sit next to me.

It wasn't exactly a bonding experience. There was no giggling, no deep, needful discussion, no nothing. I sat there and she colored me in. And I must say she stayed well within the lines.

Thirty minutes later we went downstairs. The sight of me caused my husband to choke on his coffee, sending brown spittle flying across the tabletop.

"That bad?" I asked.

"No, no, honey," he said, trying to compose himself. "You look . . . well, you look . . . great . . . I mean, different, but . . . great."

"You look like Bozo the Clown," Nadine offered.

"Nadine, don't be cruel," Cheryl said. "It was the best I could do with what I had."

I knew she wasn't talking about a limited supply of makeup. There had been no shortage of jars and pots of this and that on her counter. No, she was talking about me.

I went to the mirror in the bathroom off the kitchen and looked at myself. Nadine had been right. I turned back to the kitchen and saw a gleam in Cheryl's eye and a smirk on her perfect lips.

The capital "B" was still very plainly in sight. I went upstairs and washed my face.

"I want sand crabs to eat little holes in her flesh," I said. "I want to set fire to her hair."

"Eloise —" Liz started.

"I want to remove her teeth one by one without the use of anesthetic —"

"Eloise —"

"I want to hold her down and stuff her mouth with donuts and Twinkies!"

Liz patted my arm. "Are you through?"

"No! I want one hour in her closet with scissors and a can of lighter fluid!"

Liz laughed.

"I want to inject her thighs with cellulite!"

"She's a bitch," Liz said. "You've always known that. Knowing she's a 'special' bitch shouldn't change all that much."

"I want to —"

"Stop. You're going to drive yourself crazy. She's not really worth it, Eloise."

"Damnit, she's my sister!" I whined.

Liz shrugged. "So what? A biological accident. Us being sisters doesn't mean there's some unique bond that can never be broken — all for one and one for all. Maybe with some people it *is* like that, but it's never been with us. Honey, you've got to face up to that. This whole trip was Mother's idea because she never had sisters and she's always had some *Little Women* fantasy about how the four of us were supposed to relate to each other. Well, I'm not Jo and you're not Meg and Cheryl certainly isn't Beth."

"Beth's the one who died, right?" I said. "Please, can Cheryl be Beth?"

"When we leave here, Eloise, we'll all go back to our respective lives and only see each other every other Christmas, if then."

I felt a little twinge when Liz said that. I'd thought for a moment I had bonded with at least my oldest sister.

"We're getting along better," I said, looking at my hands.

"You and me?" She laughed. "Yeah, I guess we are. There's nothing like a common enemy to bring people together."

"But it's not real?" I asked, finding myself suddenly shy around her.

Liz shrugged. "Maybe it is. I don't know. I know Nadine and I used to be close. Up until she dumped John and took up with everybody's favorite lesbian." She ruffled my hair, just like a big sister should. "Maybe we should stay in touch more," she said.

I wanted that more than was reasonable.

"Maybe we should," I said.

Spending all my energy on Cheryl was a catch-22 situation: The more time I spent on Cheryl the less time I spent on the murder; the less time I spent on the murder, the longer we would stay on the island; the longer we stayed on the island, the longer I'd have to deal with Cheryl.

So, I told myself, forget about the Bitch. Focus on finding out what happened to Tracy Bishop. And then go home and forget you have more than two sisters.

But the memories kept popping up when least expected.

The four of us sat around the coffee table, the Monopoly board spread out in front of us, Mother's large crystal ashtray that usually adorned the table placed on the floor. Cheryl was the bank and she wasn't happy about it. Liz was usually the bank but, as eldest, had delegated the responsibility.

"I'm always the bank! It's time somebody else is

the bank! Cheryl, you do it!"

Cheryl looked aghast. "Me? I don't wanna be the bank!"

"Well, you are," Liz had declared and that appeared to be that. It was Saturday night and Liz had been grounded to the house for some violation or other, and she wasn't happy. That her unhappiness was being taken out on the three of us was not lost on any of us.

The game progressed. I was the sportscar, as I always was, and thirty minutes in I had a hotel and two houses. I was up by one house and a couple of grand.

Cheryl landed on Park Place, where my hotel stood. And she owed me big time.

"You owe me five hundred and eighty-two dollars," I declared.

Cheryl looked at the money in front of her — her own and the bank's. It seemed like forever, but it was probably only seconds, before she upended the board and ended the game. "This game sucks!" she declared and ran from the room.

When I remembered that incident, the few times I even thought about it, it was just another example of Cheryl's bitchiness. I'm winning and she quits. But had it been more than that? Had Cheryl been embarrassed because she couldn't count the money? How much of what made Cheryl Cheryl had been caused by an easily corrected physical problem? And was it too late?

I was in our bedroom, sitting on the bed

thinking these deep thoughts, when Lorrette knocked on the door and stuck her head in. "You have a phone call," she said.

A phone call? But that would be on the land phone downstairs. I'd been waiting over a day to get a call back from Luna on my cellular. Now here she is calling me on the land line where everybody and her sister (mine) would be within hearing distance.

I headed downstairs to the kitchen. Luckily, it was empty. I could see Arlan and Cheryl on the deck. Larry and Willis were in the pool, Liz sitting on the side, her legs dangling in the water, calling out rude comments to the men. Lorrette had stayed upstairs after giving me my message; I could only hope that Nadine was with her in their room.

I picked up the phone. "Hello?"

"You owe me more than toilets!" Luna said. "I'm throwing in taking out the garbage and I only wish we had septic tanks in Black Cat Ridge, because if we did —"

"Why didn't you call me on the cell phone?" I demanded.

"Because I can't! It won't go through! There's no service from the States there —"

"But I called you —"

"Yes, and I explained that to the overseas operator, but she said I still couldn't put through a call to your cell phone. I got this number from Vera. And we're on my dime now so let's hurry this up."

"I'll pay you back —"

"You bet your sweet ass you'll pay me back! Okay, I talked to Pearson, that Houston cop. He's a jerk, but a cooperative jerk. He said he didn't find much in Bishop's apartment, but he did find her mother's address and phone number. You want it?"

"Just a second," I said, grabbing for something to write on. "Shoot," I said.

She read off the address and phone number. The mother did live in Galveston, just as Liz had thought. "He notified the mother. Nothing in the apartment to shed any light on anything, he said."

"Well, now what?" I asked.

"I'm outa here," she said.

"Whoa! Wait, Luna! Did he give you any history on the girl?"

"Like what?" she asked.

"High school, anything like that?" I asked, hoping I'd at least be able to clear up Lorrette's problem.

"Why would he tell me that?" she asked.

Why indeed? She said goodbye without any fanfare and hung up.

Willis came into the kitchen, dripping pool water.

"We're going snorkeling," he said, throwing my bag of snorkel gear at me. "And I will brook no argument."

"Cool," I said, and ran upstairs to the bathroom where my swimsuit was hanging up to dry. The crotch was still wet; strangely enough that wasn't a totally unpleasant sensation.

We got in the Suzuki without telling anyone we were even leaving and, checking the map, headed to the southern tip of the island, to Salt Pond Bay, where we found a secluded beach. It was a long walk from where we had to park the car to the beach itself, but it was well worth it; unlike Cinnamon Bay Beach and the other beaches closer to Cruz Bay, this little beach was deserted. Willis and I had it all to ourselves, except for the sailboats and motor-boats farther out in the bay.

I put on my equipment, leaving my reef walkers on the sand as I donned my swim fins, and headed into the water. I could feel the light tickle of marine life all around me and looked forward to sticking my goggles in the water and becoming part of it.

I went out about waist deep, walking through a seagrass bed and over shaving brush plants, sinking into the water up to my shoulders then lying flat, using my fins to work my way a little deeper into the bay. Willis was within arm's reach, the way I liked him, and I stuck my face in the water, becoming one with the beauty of the deep.

The shallows were awash with brain, staghorn, and pillar coral. Small, brightly colored tropical fish swam in and out of the coral, followed occasionally by larger, just as brightly colored fish. Underwater flowering plants waved gently in the water as I floated on top, staring down at a world I could only glimpse, but never share.

A turtle, smaller than the one we'd seen a few days before, swam by, its jerky, awkward movements comic relief to the beauty I was watching. Willis grabbed my arm, indicating with his free hand that we follow the turtle. I agreed and we slowly set off in his wake, going deeper into the bay.

I brought out my waterproof, plastic legend of island water life and I held it in my hand as we moved through the water, trying to identify the different species of coral and fish and vegetation. There was a basket sponge, here what I was pretty sure was moon jelly, there a barracuda? Certainly not? I grabbed Willis's arm and pointed; he pulled up, studied the creature, then pointed at my legend: a gentle tarpon. I heaved a sigh of relief that went straight up my snorkel and out into the great world above.

We moved further into the bay in the wake of the turtle, although he was slowly gaining quite a lead. I slowed as I saw what was surely a sea fan with attached flamingo tongue — a great waving, blue-gray vegetation with tiny barnaclelike, coral-colored flamingo tongue attached. I waved at Willis and pointed to my legend and to the gently waving sea fan. He nodded, more intent on the turtle than on vegetation, then did a slow-motion, underwater double-take, twisting back around and grabbing my arm. He pointed frantically at the sea fan then started pulling me to the surface.

As I was being hauled up, I took one last look at the sea fan. Except maybe that wasn't what it was. The legend didn't say anything about sea fans coming equipped with arms, legs, and a gently bobbing head.

We were more than a quarter of a mile out and I could feel the beginning of panic. I wasn't that strong a swimmer.

"We've got to mark this area for the captain!" Willis yelled at me.

I nodded my head and thought better of it when the small movement caused me to go underwater.

I came back up with Willis's help, sputtering and spitting salt water. "I've got to get in!" I said. "Now, Willis!"

He must have seen the panic that was no doubt in my eyes. He eyeballed the shore for a landmark, then rolled me on my back. "Relax, honey," he said. "Just use the fins a little, then rest. Float a little, swim a little."

"I'm going to die," I said.

"No, you're not," he said. "I'm here. I haven't let you die yet, have I?"

With all we'd been through together, he definitely had a point. I tried to relax, doing as he instructed — floating a little, swimming a little.

Finally, after what seemed an interminable length of time, we got in close enough to stand.

I took off the fins and waded, splashing, falling, and bitching, up to the beach where I collapsed in a heap.

Willis sat staring out to sea.

"What was it, honey?" I asked him.

"Another frigging dead body," he said, his voice resigned.

"Could you tell who?" I asked.

He shook his head, but wouldn't look at me. "Honey?" I asked, touching his shoulder. "What's wrong?"

"Nothing. I just can't look away from the spot or I'll lose it," he said. "You go back to the car and drive to the nearest phone and call the captain. I'll stay here."

"And stare out to sea?" I asked.

"Don't mock me, woman," my husband said. "It's the only thing I can think of."

"Okay, here's the thing," Nadine said. "It's your destiny."

"Do what?" I asked, drinking thirstily from my second, or maybe my third, raspberry rum-runner.

"What are the chances that you and Willis would go to *that* beach? Huh? Million to one."

"More like a hundred to one, considering the number of beaches on the island," Liz said.

"Whatever," Nadine said, waving her off. "Hundred to one. Okay. That beach? Why? That exact direction? You think the turtle was in on it? I'm telling you, Eloise, this whole

192

finding dead bodies thing is a gift from He's directing you. Isn't it obvious?"

I nodded my head. Seemed to be.

"You sure it's God and not the devil?" I asked, always willing to play, excuse the expression, devil's advocate.

"You're saying I'm possessed by an evil demon?" I asked my big sister.

"Bullshit!" Nadine said loudly, then shushed herself and reached for the pitcher of rum-runners. "You have an angel on your shoulder, that's what you have! Because you do good with this information, right, Eloise? Not evil, right, Eloise?"

"Damn right," I said.

"See?" Nadine shouted at Liz, then shushed herself again. "Good, Liz, not evil. Our baby sister works for good!"

"Did you ever think," asked Liz, who, although decidedly tipsy, was still far less drunk then either Nadine or myself, "that our baby sister is just always in the wrong place at the wrong time?"

"Divine intervention!" Nadine shouted.

It had been an interesting day. It took me almost half an hour to get to the car and find a place to phone the captain. I didn't realize I was driving down the really wrong side of the road until I met another car, whose blaring horn got me onto the right wrong side of the road. Because we were all the way across the island at Salt Pond Bay, it took the captain an-

other half hour to find us. I waited at the car so I could take him down to the beach where Willis sat staring, hopefully, at the spot where we'd found the body.

To say Captain Robinson was ungracious is putting it mildly. He was downright hostile.

"Another dead body?" he said, his words indicating he thought that I was personally responsible for putting said body where it was, if I was even telling the truth about that.

I led him down to Willis where, again, the captain was not particularly gracious. Finally, he said, in a very snippy tone, "Will you at least look at me when I talk to you, mon?"

"Can't," Willis said. "If I take my eyes off the water, I'll lose where we saw the body."

"You didn't mark it?" the captain asked, incredulous.

"No," Willis said, gritting his teeth in an effort, I do believe, to keep from swinging around to confront the captain and thereby losing sight of the spot. "Could you please call in a boat or something so we can go out there?"

The captain did, which took another hour. Willis stared morosely at the spot the entire time. I rubbed his neck and patted his back. He didn't seem unduly appreciative.

Finally the boat came. The skipper was a gnarled old black man with white hair, leathery skin, and no teeth. That and his heavy Island patois made him totally impossible for Willis and me to understand. The captain, Willis, and

myself got aboard, Willis directing the skipper to the spot.

Needless to say, he was a little off. It took him and the skipper, both diving in circles from either side of the boat, another half an hour to find what I had initially thought was a sea fan because of the gently floating blue-gray material of the clothing worn by the body.

When they brought it up, with the captain's approval and direction, it proved most certainly not to be a sea fan. Unfortunately, it was Bud George. A little grayer and not quite as hale and hardy as the last time I'd seen him, and wearing a very noticeable new hole in the center of his forehead, but Bud George nonetheless.

TEN

Then, of course, there was the search for Marge George. No one in our party knew where the Georges had gone when they left our house in a huff after my accusatory remark to Bud, which displeased the captain to no end. This, again, was entirely my fault. No one in our group, including my turncoat husband, was man enough to disagree with the captain's appraisal of the situation.

There were many hotels on the island, but even more daily and weekly rentals of houses, apartments, campsites, boats, trailers, what have you. They could have gone anywhere. The captain elicited — make that demanded — our help in making calls to the various hotels and rental agencies. After several hours, there was still no news on the whereabouts of Marge George. The captain left in a huff, which seemed to be his general attitude when around anyone in our party.

As far as I was concerned, there were only three likely scenarios: Marge George was either dead, like her husband, from the same killer and floating fanlike somewhere in the depths of the Caribbean; on the run from having killed her husband herself; or sitting in some unknown rental spot vainly awaiting her husband's return. That, of course, didn't narrow things down any, but I felt it was succinctly put.

After an afternoon of finding yet another dead body, of being alternately glowered at and grilled by Captain Robinson, of making untold numbers of useless phone calls in search of Marge George, the pitchers of raspberry rum-runners were not so much an indulgence as a necessity.

Cheryl and Arlan had gone to their room to mourn their friend Bud George, both somehow coming to the conclusion that his death was entirely my fault; Larry and Willis were in the kitchen discussing the preferred way to pull dead bodies out of the water; and Lorette was lying down in her room with a cold compress, which left Liz, Nadine, and me free to finish off as much rum as possible while we sat on the deck, feet dangling in the pool, and discussed my penchant for discovering dead bodies.

"Willis says it's my hobby," I informed my sisters.

"Hobby schmobby," Nadine said. "It's a calling."

"Hobby schmobby?" Liz repeated and giggled.

"Nuts to you," Nadine said and pushed Liz

in the pool. She landed on her feet, her drink well out of the water, which was the main thing after all.

Liz swayed in the pool's gentle current. "Why would anyone *want* to find dead bodies?" she demanded.

Nadine rolled her eyes and sighed heavily, covering her mouth when a ladylike burp escaped. "Who said she *wants* to find dead bodies? I didn't say that! I said it's a calling! There is a difference. Jeez."

"I was referring," Liz said with great dignity, "to Willis's accusation that this is Eloise's hobby. Try to focus, Nadine, for God's sake."

"You focus!" Nadine said, using her foot to splash water in Liz's general direction. " 'Sides," she insisted, "it's Eloise's calling!"

I felt like I was at a tennis match, my head swiveling from one sister to the other as they volleyed my avocational dalliances between them.

"A calling, my ass," Liz said from the water. "A calling is like religious! Or, you know, like theatrical. I know people who feel they've been *called* to the stage! But being called to find dead bodies? Give me a break!"

"How else do you explain it?" Nadine demanded.

"It's evil," Liz said, finishing off her drink and moving in slow motion through the water to retrieve the pitcher. "I think she's possessed by the devil. You know, like Linda Blair."

Nadine turned to me. "Does your head ever rotate?" she asked me, frowning.

I shook said appendage. "I'd have noticed," I said.

"You'd think," Nadine agreed.

Liz shook her head and glared at us. "Your head doesn't have to rotate for you to be possessed," she said, seriousness ebbing from her body like the smell of booze. "Do you feel that you are sometimes led by an unseen force and then, POW, there it is, a dead body?" she asked me.

I thought about it for a moment. "I don't think so," I said.

Nadine frowned. "Well, that leaves out divine intervention, along with possession."

"You think maybe it just happens?" I asked.

They both shrugged. "Could be," Nadine said, while Liz chimed in, "It's possible, I suppose."

Willis and Larry wandered out to the deck.

"What are you girls talking about?" Larry asked.

Nadine rolled her eyes at his use of the word "girls" while I corrected him, saying strongly, "Women, Larry. Women. We are women, hear us roar."

Nadine burst into a fit of giggles. Liz laughed so hard she lost her footing and went under water, one arm held straight up in the air, saving what was left of her rum-runner.

"They're drunk," Willis said to Larry.

"You think?" Larry said, smiling.

"Good possibility," Willis said.

Larry raised an eyebrow at Willis and Willis raised an eyebrow back, then they both leered at the three of us.

"They think they're going to get lucky," I told Liz.

"Lucky, my ass," she said, and reached up out of the pool for her husband's bare leg. She jerked, pulling him into the water, which somehow got Nadine and me standing and running after Willis, who was taking off for the house.

Sometime after that I fell asleep on the couch.

I awoke to the smell of steaks on the barbecue pit. Luckily, the men were in charge, as at least three of the five women in our group were too hung over to do any serious cooking.

We ate on the deck — steak, shrimp, a big salad, and locally made French bread. We found some Ben & Jerry's Wavy Gravy ice cream, that one incredible flavor unavailable in Texas, for some obscure and ridiculous reason. Afterwards, we coupled up and watched the stars, Nadine and Lorrette paddling around in the pool together, Cheryl on Arlan's lap in a deck chair, Willis and I somehow managing to share a chaise, and Larry and Liz standing at the wall, their arms around each other, gazing off at the bay.

This was exactly the way the week should have gone from day one. This was what paradise was for — falling in love all over again. Being easy in the company of friends and family, worrying about nothing more than whether the blender will hold out for the duration and if you have enough sunscreen.

We hadn't paid over two thousand dollars a couple to worry about dead bodies and blown-up boats. We hadn't come all this way to have an island policeman accuse us as a group of wreaking havoc on his island. We hadn't left our children to the care of others to wonder if we'd ever be able to get back to them, or if we'd wind up in a prison in paradise.

None of this had been in the plan. Then again, I'd never planned it for any part of my life. But like my sisters had brought up earlier, finding dead bodies did seem to be my destiny.

Why me? Why couldn't I have been picked as the one to write the great American novel? Or to sing the "Star-Spangled Banner" at an all-Texas Superbowl? Or to paint the Sistine Chapel? Why did my destiny have to include finding dead bodies?

It wasn't fair. I was a good person. I paid my taxes, went to church on occasion, tried to teach my children to be polite. I gave to charities, voted whenever the polls were open, and called my mother every Sunday. I've never stolen anything in my life — if you don't include that time in junior high when I walked out of a store with a forty-five of "I'm Henry the Eighth, I Am" without paying. I did get caught by my mother and had to take it back and apologize. I've never intentionally hurt another living soul — except, of course, for that guy who broke into the house and tried to kill me and my kids. I beat him senseless with a butcher-block knife holder and he was hospitalized for over a week, but I think that's acceptable. And I hardly ever tell a lie. So why me?

I snuggled closer to Willis, knowing there really wasn't an answer and not expecting to get one.

We had two more days in paradise. What was going to happen on Monday if Tracy Bishop's killer hadn't been found? Not to mention Bud George's killer. One could only hope they were one in the same, but who ever really knew? If we found Tracy's, would we still be stuck on the island until Bud's killer was found? Or vice versa? I decided finding Marge would help a lot on at least some level.

I sat up. "We have to find Marge," I told the assembled group.

"We tried," Lorrette said. "It didn't get us anywhere."

"She'd be sitting right here with us if you hadn't been so rude," Arlan remarked.

I felt Willis moving to my defense and I patted him back down. "Stuff it, Arlan," I said.

"Oh, shut up, Eloise. I think everyone's had enough of you!" Cheryl said.

"You shut up, Cheryl!" Liz said. "Permanently!" She moved toward our beautiful sister, but Larry caught her by the waist and pulled her back.

"Hey, y'all," I said. "Let's simmer down. All I'm saying is we need to find Marge. I don't think the captain's going to let us go Monday if there's no word on who killed Tracy Bishop, and I think there's a possibility whoever killed Tracy also killed Bud. And if I'm right about that, then Marge could be in trouble."

"How do you figure that?" Nadine asked.

I explained the three-part scenario I'd come up with earlier: Marge was (1) dead like her husband, from the same killer; (2) on the run from having killed her husband herself; or (3) sitting somewhere innocently awaiting her husband's return.

"However," I said, "if she's not already dead, and if she didn't kill Bud herself, then she may know who did kill Bud or at least why he was killed. Which would lead to who killed him. And if she knows this, then she's in trouble. She's probably the next person on the killer's hit list."

"It's that nigger," Arlan said, "the one who put sugar in my gas tank. Gotta be."

"Arlan, watch your mouth!" Nadine said. "I don't appreciate the language."

"Oh, touch you, Ms. Hairy Lesbo!" Arlan shot back.

Obviously, my husband had had enough. He

stood up. "Arlan," he said, picking his words carefully. "Shut your mouth. You are a foul asshole and every time you open your mouth, something stinking comes out of it! And if I hear you call Nadine or Lorrette names one more time, I'm personally going to throw your ass in the ocean."

Larry laughed outright and Liz and I applauded. Nadine, however, said, "I don't need any man defending me —"

Simultaneously, Lorrette and I said, "Shut up, Nadine."

"Do you really think poor Marge is in danger?" Cheryl asked, strangely enough the one person to stay on track.

"Yeah, I'm afraid I do," I said.

There was silence in the group. Finally, Larry said, "Then we'd better find her."

"That's all I'm saying," I confirmed.

"Maybe we should start by finding that nig— that colored guy," Arlan said.

I looked at Willis. We hadn't told the group of our discovery — that the young man who had been spying on us and wreaking so much havoc was somehow related to Tracy Bishop. And that we had his name. Having his name meant we might be able to find him.

"Willis and I will do that — look for that guy who's been bothering us. Meanwhile, y'all look for Marge."

"Where?" Nadine asked. "Under the bed? In the closets?"

"St. John is not a big island," I said, "and three quarters of it is uninhabitable. She's got to be somewhere. We'll take one car, y'all split up in the other two and let's see what we can do."

"It's almost ten o'clock!" Nadine groused.

Lorrette stood up. "Then you stay here and get your beauty rest, Nadine. I'll go with Liz and Larry."

Nadine stood up. "Oh, for crying out loud."

We grabbed car keys and headed upstairs.

Jacob Bishop had not gone back to the French bistro where we'd found him, and the waiter there wasn't sure where he lived.

"I think he was rooming with Terry Macomb for a while. He might know where he is."

"Where can we find Terry?" Willis asked.

"He works at Skinny Legs in Coral Bay," the waiter told us.

We hopped back in the Suzuki and headed east to Coral Bay.

Skinny Legs Bar and Grill was a huge open-air bar surrounded by souvenir shops. Willis had to keep reminding me we were there on a mission. They had really great prices and this pair of bookends of an island cottage . . . Anyway, we found someone who knew Terry Macomb, but not Terry himself.

"No, mon, Terry he not working tonight," the bartender said.

"Actually, we're really looking for a former

roommate of his," I said, smiling brightly at the bartender. "We're friends of his mother back home. Do you know Jacob Bishop?"

"Jacob? Sure. He don' live with Terry no more. He got him a woman over to Calabash Boom, but maybe you don't tell his mother dat," the man said and laughed.

I made a face. "Better not," I said, in unspoken conspiracy. "Where in Calabash Boom?"

He gave us directions in clicks and obscure landmarks, and we headed down the dark, narrow roads toward Calabash Boom. It was less than ten miles from Skinny Legs to Calabash Boom, but it took us over an hour to find the right turnoff to Jacob Bishop's house.

It was an ancient Air Stream trailer, the aluminum still shiny in the moonlight, with an equally ancient Toyota pick-up parked in front. Huge trees dwarfed the trailer and there was the murmur of livestock from a pen in front of the house. An outdoor shower with a multicolored curtain was off to the side. As we got out of the car and headed for the small deck in front of the trailer, we could see in the pen. Four long-eared goats studied us as we went up the steps.

A dog lay on the deck. He raised his head lazily as we walked past him, sniffed us once, decided we were friendly, and laid his head back down.

There were no lights on inside the trailer

when we knocked on the door, but since it was past eleven o'clock at night I wasn't sure that meant no one was home. The Toyota pick-up seemed to indicate someone's presence.

A light flicked on inside, then the porch light came on, illuminating Willis and me as we stood on the deck. The front door opened and Jacob Bishop stood there looking at us.

"Shit!" he said, and tried to slam the door, but Willis's size-thirteen foot was already in the way.

"We need to talk, Jacob," Willis said.

"I already said everything I got to say to you people!" he said, and ran farther inside the trailer. Willis followed him.

I heard the sound of another door and ran around the side of the Air Stream. Some friends of my parents had had one of these when I was a kid, and I knew this model probably had a back door by the bedroom.

Sure enough, Jacob Bishop was coming out the back door as I rounded the trailer. I jumped on him, piggy-back style, and we both went down hard on the wet grass. Willis banged out the back door and stood over the two of us.

"E.J., just sit on him until he answers my questions," Willis said.

"You have a real mean streak, don't you, honey?" I asked.

Jacob grunted, trying to catch his breath. I shifted so he could breathe easier.

"Why did you kill Bud George?" Willis demanded.

"What?" Jacob shouted, almost toppling me over as he reared up at the question. "I didn't kill anybody! You people are the killers around here. Woman, would you get off me?" He bucked me off and we both sat on the ground, trying to catch our breath.

"We didn't kill Tracy," I said. "Her body was found in our rental house, but we didn't kill her."

He glared at me, the look quite visible in the bright moonlight.

Finally he looked at Willis. "Bud George is dead?" he asked.

"Yeah. Shot in the head and thrown in the water off Salt Pond Bay. What do you know about it?"

Jacob laughed. "Know about it? Man, I didn't even know the son of a bitch was dead. Not that I care. Best thing that could happen to the world, having that man out of it."

"How did you know Bud?" I asked. "What was he to you? And what was Tracy to you?"

He looked at me but then addressed his replies to Willis. "Tracy's my sister, man. My big sister. And you people killed her. Maybe not you two, but somebody in your house killed my sister!"

"What did Bud have to do with this?" I asked.

Jacob shook his head. "I'm not sure. But he's one of the bad guys, I can tell you that. He had Tracy into something bad — him and that ugly wife of his."

"Do you know where she is?" I asked. "His wife?"

Jacob was silent.

"Jacob, I know you've been watching our house. That's pretty damned obvious. Were you watching when Bud and Marge left yesterday? Did you see where they went?"

Still he was silent.

Willis grabbed the young man by the neck. "Talk or I swear to God I'm going to lose what little control I have left!"

"Yeah, well, try something with me, man, and I'll wipe the fucking floor with you!"

"Okay, you two," I interpreted. "Let's put the macho away for a little while. Jacob, if you didn't kill Bud George, then there's a good chance whoever killed Tracy also killed Bud. And we're afraid that that same person might be after Bud's wife. We need to find her before the killer does. Marge knows something and I'd like to find out what it is."

For the first time Jacob Bishop looked directly at me. "Yeah, me, too. You think she knows who killed Tracy?"

"I don't know, maybe. But if Tracy was into something bad with Bud George, and I seriously doubt it was something sexual —"

At that point Jacob made a very rude sound.

"Then Marge was probably in on it, too."

Jacob nodded his head. He was silent for a moment, then started to stand up. Willis grabbed him but Jacob shrugged him off. "I'll

209

take you to her," he said, heading for the pick-up.

We followed Jacob in the Suzuki. He crept over mountains and down winding trails, and took a shortcut through an area forbidden for rental cars (even four-wheel drives weren't allowed off road, according to the rental agreement). We chugged up and down ruts and crevices, Willis throwing the car into four-wheel drive, very much against rental rules. If you won't tell, we won't.

Fifteen minutes later we pulled up in front of an A-frame cabin made of wood — something you didn't see often in rentals in St. John due to the proliferation of termites. To prove the point, there was a termite hill about three feet high only yards from the front door of the A-frame.

It was after midnight but the A-frame had lights burning in the windows. We were only steps behind Jacob when he reached the door and banged on it with his fist, shouting, "Hey, old woman! Open the door! Now!"

Willis pushed him away and rapped more gently. "Marge, it's Willis and E. J. Pugh. Arlan and Cheryl's family. Remember us? We need to talk to you. It's very important."

There was no sound inside the cabin. Willis tried the doorknob but it was locked.

I moved away from the two standing by the door and went to the front window and looked in. The A-frame certainly didn't match the luxury of the cabin cruiser the Georges had rented earlier. The furniture was mismatched and badly worn, the floor linoleum, and the light came from a bare bulb hanging from the ceiling. It was one large room with a kitchen at the back and a set of rickety-looking stairs leading to a loft bedroom area. A painted and peeling railing ran the length of the loft, with posts set at about one-foot intervals.

A head full of bushy blond hair in dire need of conditioning was stuck between two of the posts, and it wasn't moving.

ELEVEN

I ran back to the porch where Willis and Jacob were arguing about how best to get in the A-frame.

"I found her!" I said.

Neither paid any attention to me as they stood their ground on the issue of whether to kick the door in or go around to the back of the house.

"Shut up!" I finally shouted. The two looked at me as if I were being rude. "I found her!" I said.

They both ran to the window and I pointed to the railing of the loft.

"Oh, shit," Willis said.

Jacob didn't say anything. He was, actually, unusually quiet even for him — until I heard the rumble of the old Toyota pick-up's engine.

Willis whirled around and ran after him, but Jacob was gone.

"We've gotta call the captain," he said, coming back to stare in the window.

"What if she's still alive?" I asked.

We both turned and stared at the A-frame.

Willis sighed and moved toward the front door. Raising his left leg, he drew back and kicked. The door splintered easily and caved in.

We both headed up the stairs to the landing where Marge lay. I grabbed her wrist and felt for a pulse. "It's weak, but it's there," I told him.

Willis looked around for a telephone, finding one on the bedside table. He quickly placed a call to the captain, asking for an ambulance.

Willis and I stood around like so much excess baggage. I was all for leaving the scene, but the only words Captain Micha Robinson had uttered to my husband and me were, "Don't move."

I needn't tell you that the captain wasn't exactly happy to see us standing guard over Marge George's prostrate body. Basically he didn't speak to us at all. He spoke to the ambulance personnel and got Marge to the hospital. He sent a flunky to tell us to follow the ambulance.

It seemed to take forever to get back to Cruz Bay. We couldn't exactly follow the ambulance since the driver was going some ungodly speed like thirty-five or forty. Willis pushed it to twenty and we managed to arrive well after the ambulance.

It was a small but well-equipped hospital. I stood outside the door to the operating room where they were working on Marge George,

213

trying to remove a bullet that had lodged somewhere near the base of her brain. Willis was
down the hall on the payphone, calling the
house to tell the rest of the family what was
going on.

"Cheryl and Arlan are on their way," Willis
told me, coming back from his phone call. "According to Cheryl, the others went out to
breakfast on the assumption that Marge has to
eat and therefore they might find her at the restaurant of their choice. I don't think Cheryl believed them. She said she'd leave a note, telling
them to meet us here."

We sat down on a bench by the door to the
OR and held hands, waiting for my sister and
her husband, or the bad news — which, of
course, when you think about it, were just
about one and the same.

By dawn, we were all gathered in the small
corridor outside the operating room. We were a
quiet bunch for vacationers. I could see the
captain down the hall, talking to a nurse and
paying no attention to us.

Nadine finally broke the silence. "What do
you think happened?" she asked, the question
directed at me.

"Somebody shot her," I said, not too graciously. "Presumably the same person who shot
Bud."

"What do you think her chances are, honey?"
Lorrette asked Nadine.

Nadine shrugged. "It depends on where the bullet lodged. How deeply it went in, what kind of round it was. Some do more damage than others. But the fact that she's still alive is a good sign."

Well, there was no arguing with that logic. And to think the woman had a master's in nursing.

Finally, a doctor came out of the OR, thankfully wearing clean scrubs. Captain Robinson rushed to join us.

"It's going to be touch and go," the doctor said, addressing his comments mostly to Nadine, as she had introduced herself as an RN. "We got the bullet and stopped the hemorrhaging, but she's unconscious." He shrugged. "Whether she wakes up from the anesthetic or not is anybody's guess. A trauma like that often causes severe brain damage, coma, eventual death." He shrugged again. "It's a wait-and-see game right now, I'm afraid."

"I'll keep a guard by her door, Doctor," the captain said. Addressing the rest of us he said, "You people go on home now." Then he looked at Willis and me. "Except you two. You come to my office now."

He turned on his heels and was gone. The others glanced guiltily at us then scurried for their cars and home. Willis and I, as usual, were on our own.

I was exhausted. It was after two o'clock in the morning and I hadn't had any sleep since my alcohol-induced coma of the afternoon. I was hot, bug-bit, hungry, and ready for bed, but there was obviously no way I was going home until the captain had had his say.

We got in the car and headed to the station, where we waited for over an hour before Captain Robinson showed up. There was a slight smear of dried egg on his neatly pressed khaki shirt. As neat as the captain usually was, I had a feeling he'd dropped food on himself on purpose, just to piss me off. If that had been his plan, he succeeded beautifully.

We stood up when he came in the door.

"Sit down," he said, taking his seat in the chair at the desk. "I got another fax from your police chief Catfish Watkins," the captain said. "He said you're not a criminal but that you're a very big busybody and always sticking your nose in police business. Is that what you're doing here, Mrs.? If it is, I think maybe you should stop it before someone chops your nose off!"

I shrugged expansively. "These things just happen to me, Captain," I tried to explain. "I don't really try —"

"Hush," he said. He looked at Willis. "You American men don't know how to keep your women in line, sir. I would suggest a whip, but you might think me crude."

Willis was silent. The only responses appropriate to that remark would have gotten him in Dutch with either the captain or me, and

Willis, although not always the brightest bulb in the pack, is no fool.

"Captain —" I started.

"Hush." He stared at me for a long moment, then sighed. "How did you find Marge George?"

Now was the time to tell the captain everything — about Jacob Bishop, his relationship to Tracy, his suspicion of the Georges, and his running away.

I took a deep breath and told all.

When I finished, the captain glared at me. The room was deathly silent for so long I had an overpowering urge to start babbling, but I held my tongue.

Finally, Captain Robinson sighed. "Why didn't you tell me all this earlier?"

"I tried to but —" I started.

He glared at Willis. "Cat got you tongue, mon? You woman always speak for you?"

Willis stood up, his fists clinched. The captain stood up, too. I stood up just so I wouldn't have to crane my neck to see what was going on. I put a restraining hand on my husband's arm, but he shook it off.

"Captain, my wife is a person in her own right. She does what she does. She's answerable only to herself. And as she was just trying to tell you — again! — we both tried to tell you earlier about Jacob Bishop but you seemed much more interested in waving that fax from Catfish Watkins in our faces than finding out

217

what the hell is going on around here! And just because I'm not a chauvinistic, fat-headed flat-foot —"

I put a hand over his mouth and smiled at the captain. "Can we go now?" I asked sweetly.

The captain shook his head. "You Americans —" he started.

"Wait a minute!" I said. "This is the *American* Virgin Islands, Captain. You're an American, too, you know!"

He straightened his shoulders and glared at me. "I'm a Virgin Islander! First and foremost! My father was an islander and my grandfather was an islander! We were islanders long before the United States decided to take us over!"

Oops, I thought. I repeated my earlier question. "May we go home now?"

He waved his hand at us. "Go! I don't care! Get out of my sight!"

As we headed for the door, he said, "And don't find any more bodies, dead or otherwise, do you hear me?"

We both nodded and got the hell out.

We stopped for breakfast, then headed up the mountain toward our home away from home. The CD player was blaring when we came in, Bob Marley telling tales of woe about buffalo soldiers. We'd noticed only the damaged Land Rover when we'd parked, still awaiting its replacement from the bigger island; the other Suzuki was gone.

I hollered hello as we came down the stairs, hoping to be heard over the blare of the stereo. Arlan and Cheryl were out on the deck, Cheryl in a shiny silver swimsuit, strawberry blond hair piled high on her head, curls haphazardly cascading over the back of the chaise. The bandolero top of the swimsuit crisscrossed her breasts, making her look even more voluptuous than usual. God, that woman was a pain in the butt.

The Toad, better known as my brother-in-law, lay in all his furry splendor on an adjoining chaise, his Speedo covering entirely too little of him.

"Where is everybody?" I asked Arlan.

"Shopping," he said. "Although why they think that's an appropriate thing to do right now, I don't know."

Ignoring his comment, I turned to Cheryl. "Any word from the hospital?"

She shook her head. "I guess no news is good news," she said and sighed, showing more compassion toward Marge George than she ever had a member of her family. "Some vacation, huh?" she said.

I gave her a wan smile. "Pretty scenery," I managed.

A tear traveled down my sister's satin-smooth cheek. "This has just been so awful!"

Arlan moved to his wife's side, while Willis said, "I'll get her a glass of water," and hightailed it into the kitchen before I had a chance to.

Then the doorbell rang. "I'll get it!" I said and headed up the stairs.

When I opened the front door at the top of the stairs, I was dumbfounded to find Jacob Bishop standing there. He was dressed, for the first time since I'd first seen him, in slacks, a shirt, and real shoes, his dredlocks pulled back and stuffed under a cap. Beside him stood Tracy Bishop.

Except she was older and darker. But with the exception of those two things, she was the spitting image of the girl I'd seen on the beach — the girl whose body Willis had dragged out of the cistern in the living room.

"Mrs. Pugh," Jacob said, "I would like to present my mother, Marie Bishop."

I held out my hand to the tall, lovely older woman. She looked at it for a split second, then took my hand in hers. "I'm so sorry for your loss, Mrs. Bishop," I said. "Won't you both come in?"

I let go of her hand and stepped back, ushering them both inside. "The living room's downstairs," I explained, heading for the stairs. "Please come down and I'll get us all some coffee."

"That's very kind of you," Mrs. Bishop said, her voice soft and low, a velvet purr.

I led them down the stairs where we met Willis coming out of the kitchen. I introduced Mrs. Bishop to my husband. Taking her hand, he reiterated what I'd said about her loss. She nodded her head very formally. "I'll get coffee," Willis said and headed back for the kitchen, forgetting the water he had in his hand for Cheryl.

As I seated our guests in the living room, Cheryl and Arlan came in from the deck. Arlan blanched at seeing Jacob sitting on one of the sofas. "What the hell is that nig— that asshole doing here?" he demanded.

Marie Bishop looked up at the rude comment. Her face paled and she stood, her body shaking.

"Oh, my God," she said. "Sweet Lord Jesus save me!"

I looked from Mrs. Bishop to my brother-in-law. Although it is hard to tell in an extremely dark-skinned person when they pale, in someone as white as Arlan Hawker, the color drain was quite apparent. It was as if all the blood rushed out of his face, leaving it tinged slightly blue; within seconds, however, the blood rushed back, painting his face a fierce scarlet, like high blood pressure about to burst an aneurysm.

"Mama?" Jacob asked, grabbing his mother as she clutched at him.

"Take me away from here, Jacob! Now!"

"Mrs. Bishop?" I asked, moving closer to her. "Are you all right? Can I get you a glass of water?"

She pointed a shaking finger at Arlan. "She found you," she said, her voice hoarse. "And you killed her!"

221

Willis came in from the kitchen with a tray laden with coffee cups just as Jacob Bishop let go of his mother and charged Arlan.

But Arlan was too quick. He grabbed Cheryl and hit the tray Willis was holding, knocking it out of Willis's hand and sending hot coffee splashing across the room and onto Willis's bare legs.

By the time we all looked back at Arlan, he had his pocketknife out and was holding the blade to Cheryl's throat. "Stay away from me, asshole!" he yelled at Jacob.

"What do I care if you kill her? She's your woman, man!" Jacob said, moving again toward Arlan. Willis grabbed Jacob and held him back.

"What the hell are you doing, Arlan?" Willis demanded.

"That's what I'd like to know!" Cheryl said, pulling at her husband's hand on her arm. "Arlan, I don't find this amusing!"

"Arlan, please," I said, trying to keep my voice calm. "Don't hurt her."

Cheryl scoffed. "For God's sake, Eloise, Arlan is not going to hurt me!"

"I'll gut her like a fish, Willis!" Arlan said "Stay back."

And to prove his words, he pushed the poir of the blade into Cheryl's skin, pricking th flesh. Blood oozed out. Cheryl touched h hand to her neck; her hand came back cover in blood.

"You goddamn son-of-a-bitch!" Chery

shouted. Her leg went back, catching her husband neatly in the balls, while one arm came out to deflect the knife. Arlan doubled over and Cheryl grabbed the knife hand and rammed the hand against her knee. Beyond the sound of the knife hitting the floor, you could hear the crunch of bone.

Willis let go of Jacob and grabbed the knife. Jacob grabbed Arlan.

I looked at my sister. "Way to go, girl," I said.

"I hope this doesn't scar," she said, heading for the bathroom mirror to check her neck.

Arlan was taken to the hospital first to set his broken arm, then to the police station by one of Captain Robinson's officers; Cheryl was on the phone in the kitchen trying to locate their lawyer back in Houston.

The others had gotten back from their "frivolous" shopping adventure — buying a nightgown, slippers, and a robe for the hospitalized Marge George — so we all gathered in the living room. The captain, Jacob Bishop and his mother Marie, Nadine, Lorrette, Liz, Larry, Willis, and me. The captain had asked Mrs. Bishop the $64,000 question: What was going on?

Mrs. Bishop held her son's hand and looked balefully into his eyes. "I am so sorry, Jacob, that you are going to hear these things. This is something a mother never wants a son to know."

"Mama," he said, gripping her hand, "it's okay. You can tell me anything, Mama, anything."

She touched her hand to his cheek, smiled at him, then turned to the captain. "My late husband Melvin Bishop was not Tracy's father." She looked at her son as he made a slight sound beside her. "When I was a young woman, I worked at a truckstop in a little bitty town in Louisiana, near my parents' home. The restaurant was owned by a black man, but most of the truckers were white. Most were okay to us, but some weren't so nice." She took a deep breath. "Arlan Hawker came in at least once a month on one of his routes. He said rude things to me, made lewd suggestions. I tried not to pay any attention to him, but one night I sassed him. The other truckers laughed."

She took Jacob's hand in hers and squeezed. "That night when I left to walk home, he was waiting for me. He beat me up and raped me."

"Mama! Did you call the cops?" Jacob demanded.

Marie Bishop shook her head. "Not back then, *cher*," she said. "A black woman didn't yell rape against a white man. Wouldn't do no good."

"Did you tell anyone?" her son demanded.

"I told my daddy and Mr. Leroy who ran the diner. They were on the lookout for him, but he musta changed his route or something; he never came back through there again. I never

224

saw him again. Until today."

"And you got pregnant with Tracy?" I asked.

Mrs. Bishop nodded. "The only good thing to come out of that horrible man," she said. She smiled. "My Tracy was a good girl."

"How did she find out?" Larry asked. "I mean, she did know, right? It wasn't just a co-incidence that she came to work for me?"

Mrs. Bishop shrugged. "I think maybe that was part of her plan — working for you. As to how she found out, she was with my daddy at the end. He told her before he died. His mind was a little messed up; he thought he was talking to me about it instead of Tracy."

"Did she confront you?" I asked.

Marie Bishop nodded. "Yes. She was very angry. I married Melvin when Tracy was a baby and he took her as his own. She never knew 'til then that Melvin wasn't her daddy. She left home and there wasn't anything I could do to stop her. She was a grown woman, after all."

"What about Marge and Bud George?" the captain asked.

Mrs. Bishop shook her head. "I don't know. She called me a couple of months back and said she found some people who were gonna help her take care of Arlan Hawker. That may have been these people. She wouldn't tell me what she planned to do. I didn't even have her phone number in Houston or her address." She looked at Larry. "She never told me who she was working for either."

The captain turned his attention to Jacob. "You came here with your sister?" he asked.

Jacob shook his head, thought better of it and said, "No, sir. I'd been on the island for six months when I got the call from Tracy. She said she wanted to come visit me. I was living with another guy then, and Tracy said to rent us a place together — that she'd pay for it, but not to tell anybody," he looked at his mother, "especially Mama, about her coming out. So that's when I rented the trailer in Calabash Boom."

"So what do you know about Bud and Marge George?" the captain demanded.

Jacob shrugged. "I saw her with both of them at different times. He even came out to the trailer once when I wasn't there. I came home just when he was leaving. Tracy wouldn't tell me what was going on, just that Bud George was helping her get her meal ticket."

"What did that mean?" the captain asked.

Again Jacob shrugged. "I don't know. She wouldn't explain."

"I think one of the people who can answer all these questions, Captain, is sitting in one of your cells right now," I said.

"Mr. Arlan Hawker," the captain said. He stood and shook his head. "And the other one, Mrs. George, may never speak again." He sighed. "But I think maybe I go talk to Mr. Hawker now. Ladies," he said, bowing slightly, mostly in Mrs. Bishop's direction. He headed

226

up the stairs. Before he reached the top, he turned and looked down at us. "Mr. Bishop," he said, "you wouldn't know anything about explosives, would you?"

Jacob Bishop didn't bat an eye. "Not a thing, Captain," he said.

"I would guess not. Or you wouldn't have rigged the bomb to go off after the Georges left the boat."

"Unless, of course, the bomb was only meant to scare them. I mean, whoever set it. That could have been their plan," Jacob said with a straight face.

The captain nodded slowly. "Could be," he said, "could be." He headed up the rest of the stairs and out the front door.

Before Jacob and his mother left, I pulled him aside. "One more question," I said.

"What's that?"

"Why did you try to kill Arlan at the Catherineberg ruins?" I asked. "Did you already suspect him?"

"Try to kill *him?*" Jacob demanded. "Shit, I should have figured that's what he'd say! That asshole was trying to kill me! I didn't even see him coming. I followed y'all, trying to keep an eye on all of you. I was standing back in the trees by the cliff. I guess he must have seen me. Next thing I know I'm half over the cliff, holding on to that creep for all I'm worth. When you screamed, you distracted him enough for me to get away. I wish now I had thrown him over, but then, lady, *he* was doing the throwing, believe me."

I patted him on the shoulder. "Strangely enough," I said, "I do."

It cost us seventy-five dollars a piece to change our departure date, but the captain needed us to stay on the island one more day.

He released Cheryl to go home and make arrangements with Arlan's lawyer, and Nadine and Lorrette were allowed to leave with her.

Strangely enough, there was a little emotional scene between my sister Cheryl and I before the ferry took the three off to the big island.

She was standing on the deck, looking out to sea, her bags all packed and stashed by the front door upstairs. She was wearing a silk shift of brightly patterned hibiscus, diamonds winking at her throat, in a vain attempt to cover the bandage over the knife nick.

I came up behind her and said, "Cheryl, I'm really sorry."

She turned and smiled a sad smile. She shook her head. "Damnedest thing, huh?"

I agreed.

"He's been a good husband, Eloise. A good father. I'm not sure I believe any of this."

"You might want to think about getting the girls some help," I said, not wanting to address Arlan's guilt or innocence with my sister.

She nodded her head. "A good idea. You

know that woman has him mixed up with someone else, don't you, Eloise?"

I sighed. "Cheryl, I don't see how."

"He's my husband," she said, a pleading sound to her voice.

"Are you okay?" I asked.

She turned and impulsively hugged me. "You really are trying, aren't you, Eloise?"

"Yes, Cheryl, I am," I said.

She nodded. "Well, we do have a bit of a past," she said.

I took a deep breath. "I'm sorry I cut your hair," I said.

She took a step back. "Wow." She laughed. "I'm sorry I locked you in the bathroom," she said.

I impulsively hugged her back. "Let's keep in touch," I said.

"Definitely," she said.

Our beautiful house was leased out to someone else so Liz, Larry, Willis, and I had to relocate. The Westin was gracious enough to give us emergency shelter, at an exorbitant rate. Our room was gorgeous, but after the house it felt a little small. We called Vera to let her know we'd be coming back a day later (which caused Bessie no undue stress, as we could hear clearly over the long distance line), then Willis called his partner, Doug Kingsley. Even though Willis had the phone to his ear and I was sitting a foot away on the bed, I could hear Doug behaving in an almost identical manner to our ten-year-old Bessie. His high stress level had something to do with a big contract and a hot date, which unfortunately were going to coincide. Doug was going to have to make a choice. Willis was rather emphatic on what choice he thought Doug should make. Personally, I wasn't taking any bets on which way he'd go.

Tuesday evening Captain Robinson found us at the beach bar, deep into our second pitcher of painkillers — a very nice drink made with several different kinds of rum. He sat down and allowed us to pour him a drink.

"Arlan talking yet?" I asked.

The captain shook his head. "That mon won't shut his mouth for nothing," he said. "I keep tellin' him, 'Mon, you lawyer's coming. Shut you mouth!' but he just keep talking!"

"And?" I prodded.

The captain took a long sip of the painkiller and grinned at me. "Catfish Watkins was right — you are a nosy woman, Mrs."

"Captain!" I whined.

"First he denies everything. Then in the same breath he says how the girl, that Tracy, she was going to bleed him dry. Then he calls the Georges names make me blush, and I been a policeman twenty-two years!" He shook his head. "Then the next breath he denies everything again. If the man just kept his mouth shut, he might get out of this — we ain't got that much evidence." He glared at me and pointed his finger. "You don't tell him I said that!"

My eyes got big. "Are you kidding? After what he did? I would not go out of my way to help him in any way, Captain, brother-in-law or not."

"I find out from Hawker and from my sources in the U.S. about the Georges. But that's not their names. Klondin's their name. Max and Rachel. And they aren't even from Texas —"

"I knew it!" I said. "They were just way too obvious!"

"They're from Wisconsin —"

"Ha!" I said, splashing a little bit of my pain-killer. "Yankees!"

The captain glared at me. "If you don't mind," he said. I nodded my head regally for him to continue.

"Got rap sheets in about ten states for fraud, check kiting, forgery, you name it. Major con artists. He's been in jail twice. She's been charged eleven times but never convicted." He shook his head. "Lovely folks."

Liz rolled her eyes. "And we had them spending the night with us! God, Larry, check your credit cards."

"Hell," Willis said, "let's all check our teeth. They may have gotten off with our gold fill-ings."

"A little dental humor, Willis?" Larry asked.

"I try," my husband said, raising his glass to

the waiter. Looked like another round of pain-killers was coming up.

On the day we were to leave for home, we got a call from Captain Robinson saying Marge George (or Rachel Klondin or whoever she was) was conscious. Willis and I made a stop by the hospital on the way to the ferry.

She was sitting up in the raised hospital bed, and her blond hair was gone, replaced by a white turban of bandages. Her face was devoid of makeup and, when she spoke, the bad Texas drawl was missing.

"The captain says I owe you my life," she said, although the look she gave me seemed to cancel out the words.

I shrugged. "You grateful enough to answer some questions?" I asked.

She smirked. "Ask me anything. I already had a talk with the federal prosecutor who's giving me quite a nice deal in exchange for my testimony against that asshole Arlan Hawker. So I have nothing to hide."

"What kind of deal?" I asked.

She smiled. "Five years probation for my testimony."

"Not bad," I said.

"Not bad at all," she agreed. She grinned at me. "Bet that really pisses you off."

"More than you'll ever know," I agreed. Changing the subject, I asked, "How did you find Tracy in the first place?"

"We didn't," she said, "Tracy found us. She dated a kid we used in a couple of schemes a while back, and when she told him about dear old daddy, he suggested she contact us." She grinned. "That girl was ready for some revenge with a capital 'R,' I can tell you that. Max — Bud — did a computer check on Hawker and found out how much he was worth, which was quite a surprise to his darling daughter, by the way. All she knew was some trucker had raped her mama and run off. Now this trucker's a big-time businessman worth a couple of mil. Well, she didn't have to ask Max and me twice, I can tell you that."

"So her whole idea was to just get money out of him?" I asked.

Marge/Rachel shook her head then winced. "Whoa, better not do that," she said. "No, her idea was to kill him. That's what she thought Max and I were going to help her do. Out of the goodness of our hearts, I suppose. Like we were some strange Lone Ranger or Robin Hood or something. We didn't set her straight. We figured the kid could do whatever she wanted once we had him set up and money in hand."

"No honor among thieves, huh?" Willis said.

Rachel laughed. "Ah, honey, that kid was no thief. She was a civilian. She wasn't the payday, but she could certainly get us to a good one." She sighed. "Who knew Arlan Hawker was gonna be that hard?" A tear formed in one eye. "I'm gonna miss Maxey, I can tell you that.

Best partner I ever had. That boy could tell a tale make you weep."

"What happened the night you were shot?" I asked.

Rachel sighed. "Oh, honey, I don't like to think about that. No, siree. Max had it all figured out. Called Arlan, told him we had proof he killed Tracy, not to mention that he was her daddy, told him how much we wanted, had the meet all set up —"

"How was Arlan supposed to get that kind of money on the island?" Willis asked.

Rachel gave him a pitiful glance. "Wire transfer, honey. Ever heard of it?"

"Oh," Willis, the high-finance whiz, said.

"Max was supposed to meet with him while I stayed at the cabin and manned the phone in case he needed me. The meet was supposed to be at midnight, but then I get a call from Max on his cell phone saying Hawker never showed up, so Max says he's coming back to the cabin. Ten minutes later I get another call, him telling me to pack up and get the hell out of the cabin, then the phone goes dead." Tears were slowly flowing down Rachel's face. "I run upstairs and grab the bags, but before I even get started, the front door slams open. I run to the railing to see if it was Max. Instead it's Arlan. And he aims a gun at me —" She was quiet for a moment. "That's the last thing I remember before waking up here."

Part of me felt sorry for her — the part that wasn't outraged by what she and her partner had put into motion in the first place. I looked at her lying in bed, her pasty face even pastier against the white sheets and white turban of bandages around her head. And for the first time I saw how truly pathetic she was. Sixty-something, having lived a life of crime, with nothing to show for it — no partner, no money, no home. "Do you have children?" I asked her.

She nodded. "Max and I have a boy. He's in Joliet right now, but he should be up for parole in three or four years . . ."

"I always thought he was scum," Liz said as we swayed atop the ferry heading for Charlotte Amalie on St. Thomas, "ever since Cheryl came home with him!"

"He certainly wasn't my favorite brother-in-law," I said.

Larry grinned. "That means I am, right?"

"I was thinking of Lorrette —" I started, but Liz hit me on the arm.

"What's Cheryl going to do now?" I asked the group at large.

Liz shook her head. "Honey, don't worry about Cheryl. She'll always land on her feet."

I turned for one long last look at St. John. The colors were still staggering — the turquoise blue sea, the darker blue sky, the green mountains, the colorful buildings holding on to the sides of the cliffs. We'd come back here, Willis and I. Maybe we'd bring the kids — or maybe we wouldn't. But we'd come back.

TWELVE

It's been eight months since the trip to paradise. Per the advice of his high-priced attorney, Arlan pled guilty to two counts of murder. In lieu of the death sentence, he was given two consecutive life sentences in a federal prison, since one of his crimes — the killing of Bud George — was done on government property; the A-frame cabin and the area around it stood on the grounds of the Virgin Islands National Park. In his confession, he claimed that he'd gone to the A-frame to confront the Georges and that Bud had pulled a gun on him. Arlan went for the gun and in the ensuing scuffle, the gun went off, hitting Marge (or Rachel) where she stood at the railing of the loft. According to Arlan, Bud then ran out of the house, leaving the gun to Arlan, who followed him and shot him, later taking the body and dumping it in the Caribbean. No one really believed this account of the events, since Marge/Rachel was in court to tell her side of the story, which differed considerably.

Two things Arlan continued to deny, however: One, that he had ever touched Marie Bishop, and two, that he'd had any intention of hurting Cheryl. I believed him about Cheryl, but a DNA test on Tracy Bishop's remains proved Arlan to be her father.

The kids loved the gifts we brought them, but Bessie didn't think they were worth the time away from her, and Vera, my mother-in-law, thought the caftan I bought her was a little risqué for her taste — although I've seen her wear it at least three times since I gave it to her.

Luna came by the day we got back with a copy of her phone bill (I won't even mention how much that turned out to cost) and a piece of paper she made me sign and had Willis witness that stated I had to clean her toilets once a week for three months and take out her garbage on a nightly basis for one month. I tried to argue my way out of it, but it didn't work. It wouldn't be so bad if she didn't have two teenage sons at home.

Liz and Larry came to Black Cat Ridge for Thanksgiving this year as their daughters and grandchildren all had plans. Larry has taken over management of Arlan's dental lab, with Cheryl's blessings, and, along with his own dental practice, is making quite a killing — if you'll excuse the expression. Liz actually read one of my books and said it wasn't bad for schlock writing. I'm thinking about stopping by her *small* theater group next time I'm in Houston.

Nadine and Lorette are talking about adopting a child, although Nadine's two sons aren't that crazy about the idea. I've invited them for Christmas; we'll see what happens.

I haven't heard from Cheryl since the day she left the island. Of course, I haven't called her either. I did hear from Mother, however, that Cheryl's divorce from Arlan is final and that she plans on marrying again for the fifth time (but who's counting?), this time to Arlan's lawyer. Just as soon as his divorce is final.

Looking back on the whole experience, I can definitely say it's left me with a good news/bad news situation: The good news is I have a new relationship with at least one of my sisters, and maybe more some day; the bad news is my mother found out about it. God only knows what she's going to come up with next.